Seth mounted and glanced ι
him. The Flatheads were streaming down towards them.
They erupted into wild war-cries, brandishing their bows,
sending their mounts in a recklessly wild plunge down the
slippery hillside.

'Run for it!' Jules yelled and bent low over his horse's neck.
They lit out by the way they had come. The pair were riding
neck-and-neck, faces taught and defiant.

Seth twisted backwards and tried to estimate the numbers
pursuing them. There were at least eight Flatheads, probably
more. Eight, nine, ten . . .

There was no time to make sure.

MOON PRAIRIE

Lauran Paine

GUNSMOKE

First published in the UK by Hamilton

This hardback edition 2008
by BBC Audiobooks Ltd
by arrangement with
Golden West Literary Agency

ISBN 978 1 405 668165 0

British Library Cataloguing in Publication Data available.

Printed and bound in Great Britain by
Antony Rowe Ltd., Chippenham, Wiltshire

CHAPTER ONE

OLD JULES looked long at the picture and delivered himself of an opinion with great deliberateness. "No woman looks like that, Seth. You see, women have got two ages. The first one's when they're young an' pretty. The other's when they git along towards thirty-five sort of. They ain't young no more, but they're a mite fuller in the chops, y'understand."

Jules looked around at the younger man to see if he was listening. He was, in a drowsy way.

"Well, whoever painted this picture went an' took a woman that's got the fullness of a mature woman, an' painted out the lines. So, here's a lady with mature beauty an' young beauty too, an' there just ain't no such woman." He paused. "I know."

The quiet in the little cabin lengthened. Was broken only by the busy sounds from the fireplace from which came waves of heat that spread throughout the room.

"Where'd you get it?"

The man called Seth turned his head a little. There was a flush to his face from the warmth. "Picked it up out of the stuff the Blackfeet left behind."

Jules grunted and worked over the dark red meat he was placing very meticulously in a big iron skillet. Bending low and squinting, he deftly caught up some coarse brownish-black hairs and flicked them aside. "You say it was a mule train? How many do you reckon was in it?"

"Oh, maybe eight or ten. Looked like they were packing settler stuff. Unusual." Seth said pensively. "Mule trains are usually traders or trappers or the like. Don't know as I ever saw immigrants use mules like that before."

"Sure it was settlers?"

"Pretty sure. The stuff the Injuns left behind wasn't trader-goods. It was dresses and the like. Household stuff and so forth."

Jules took the black old skillet to the mud and stone fireplace and put it on a stonework ledge. He straightened up when he spoke, but kept an eye on the toplash of flames where they smote the undersides of the pan. His interest in the conversation was obviously secondary. Buffalo hump steaks after a cold, wet day along the trap lines were much more vital and important to him.

"They did right, though, Seth. Wagons are out of place here. Too slow, anyway. Now, was an immigrant party smart, they'd do just that. They'd travel a-horseback. Pack what they could on big Yankee mules and go across the plains as fast as they could. Stand a lot better chance of side-steppin' Injuns."

The younger man uncoiled his lean, tawny body and stood up from the bench he'd been lolling on. He was about half the age of Jules. His dark, reddish-brown hair was sunburnt-looking, like the smooth ruddiness of his face. He had alert, rarely still, blue eyes that had a hint of animal fierceness in their depths. Only now they were troubled and therefore shades darker and still. Brooding eyes. He looked at old Jules's hawkish, seamed and weathered profile for a moment then dropped his glance to the small, oval painting of the girl's face.

Jules turned away from the fireplace at that moment and saw Seth standing there studying the picture. His dark old eyes swung down to the image then lifted quickly, dartingly, to the younger man's face. A sudden understanding, with a little abrupt surprise in it, flashed across his expressive face.

"Pretty, ain't she, boy?"

Seth looked up without answering. He nodded. Their glances held for a moment, then Jules's leathery grin came up slowly and slyly.

6

"Did they scalp her?"

"She wasn't there, Jules. That's what stumps me." Seth dropped the painting into his little beaded bag and looked puzzled. "There were five dead men. Three of 'em had been scalped."

"Only three?"

Seth nodded. "The other two were bald. The mules were gone, of course, but I read the sign. About fifteen mules and seven saddle horses."

Jules nodded too, but slowly, as though digesting thoughts and converting them into deductions with the head motion. "They took the girl and one other captive. Must've been another woman. Blackfeet don't often take grown men for prisoners. Children, yes; not men. Well— but I reckon them women are dead by now. Siksika travel fast. They're hard on prisoners anyway. How long had things been there when you come onto 'em?"

"Maybe a day. Maybe a day and a night. They went west when they left out. Funny they didn't come around here and raise a little hell if it was a war party."

Jules turned and cast a hungrily appraising glance at the frying meat. The odour was all through the little log and mud soddy-cabin, as all-pervading as the firelight. "Might've been some we know, Seth. You know how they are. Hate all white men but have a white man or two that are their friends."

Seth nodded in silence and Jules moved toward the fireplace.

The interior walls of the cabin were hung with beautiful skins of white wolves and antelope. There were two immense buffalo robes overlapping on the dirt floor and a pile of freshly oiled traps were piled carelessly in a corner near the narrow, low door. Benches were along the walls and clumsy little rawhide-slatted stools were here and there. It was a typical hutment of mountain trappers far back in the wild, isolated mountains. A massive, lone candle sweated to a laboriously made dish of steamed buffalo horn, was on the solitary table in the room. The table was so low the two men squatted cross-legged when they ate.

Jules wolfed his food and drank the tankard of blood bouillon with the steam from it running up past his glittering, small, dark eyes. He watched the deliberate way Seth ate, set the tankard down, and dragged a shiny buckskin sleeve across his mouth.

"All right, Seth," he said, as one might speak to a dog who was trying to make a wish known. "You've a notion. Out with it."

"No," Seth said, eating from the tip of his sheath knife. "I've got no notion, Jules. But I wish I'd gotten there sooner."

Jules smothered a snort and belched instead. "You'd have done nothing, boy. One against twenty, maybe. You've seen it happen before. I'm sorry it happened, just like you are, but it's done. You know, Seth, someday it won't be like this. When that day comes we won't be trappin' in here either. It's one or t'other, boy. Now we get pelts and see things we don't like. Later we'll see things that're like they're supposed to be—but we'll get no pelts." Jules looked fondly, proudly, and just a little avariciously, at the carefully baled hides stacked along the south wall of the cabin. "That's the way she be. Now, we're prosperin', Seth. Then we'll starve or hire out for dregs; do you understand?"

"Yep," Seth said, finishing his supper and fumbling in his little bag for the green-stone Blackfoot pipe with its reed stem and pungent odour. "I understand that all right, Jules, but that girl," he hesitated and flushed a little and avoided the older man's glance by working over the loading of the pipe, "was the prettiest I've ever seen."

Jules was going to speak when they both heard it at the same time. A soft, slithering sound outside, such as a moccasined foot would make. Seth was half turned facing

8

the door before the noise had died away. Slower, Jules was pushing himself up from the table by placing both hands, palms down, fingers extended, on the smooth edge, and stiffening his arms. Neither man spoke nor moved after Jules was upright and Seth had his long, fragile-looking rifle in his hands.

The sound didn't come again for a while, but when it did there was a garrulous, whining voice beyond the door. Seth put aside his rifle with a wry smile at the older man. Jules made a slashing gesture with one hand, then placed both hands before his stomach and made a circular motion —the sign-talk symbol of the Gros Ventres—which also meant Big Bellies. In this case it meant Jules knew who their guest was and was ruefully saying the man was always in time to eat.

"Bill."

Seth let him in. He was a tall, very lean, stooped man with ferret-like, small eyes that were never still and a nose that overhung his upper lip. His protruding, witch-like chin, arose to meet it, making an altogether unprepossessing appearance. The trapper's buckskins were shiny with sweat, great age and uncleanliness. His tomahawk and knife hung disconsolately from his ancient belt and his long-rifle was much scratched and nicked with the evidence of long, hard years of use as a staff, a weapon, and a shield against prickly brush and whipping tree limbs.

"Boys," the newcomer said in his reedy, whining voice, the little blue eyes roving constantly and finally alighting with slavering greed upon the remains of the hump roast, "a storm's a-comin' and a man's unwise to stay out. Hungry like he is. Figured I'd cache here with you till it's past. Hear me, boys; she's a-goin' to rain like the Missouri River jumpin' off'n the Rockies."

Seth smiled and winked at Jules. "Bill, I reckon it wasn't the smell of rain that drove you to fort up. You've quite a beak for smelling. Tell the truth. How far were you when you first caught scent of that hump roast?"

Mountain man Bill Williams looked reproachfully at Seth. Regarded him with injured feelings for a silent moment, then swung his shaggy head to behold Jules, whose smile was even wider than Seth's. "Jules, you an' me got better manners than that, ain't we? Insult a man on an empty gut. Hear me, Jules, she's a-goin' to bust loose an' flood the feet off'n the frogs. Boys, that's a big hunk o' meat. You'd feed an old pardner, I know."

With that, Bill Williams leaned his rifle against the wall and knelt at the table, drew his skinning knife and went to work.

Seth sat down and lit his pipe with a coal from the fire. "Bill, you about to head back?"

"Ain't goin' back this winter, boys," Williams said around huge mouthfuls of meat. "Wintering up at the headwaters of the Kootenai this year. I got a squaw up there'll make me new clothes." He flicked out a great, long, skinny leg and flapped a much-patched moccasin at Seth. "She's fatter'n a calfy cow buffalo, but she can make moccasins and chew down hides an' make clothes—an' cook, boys—she can cook." He went back to eating with a rhythmic sweep of his long arms and spoke without looking up again. "I'll winter in this year, boys. See you at rendezvous in the spring."

Jules looked once at the bales of rich pelts then back at Bill Williams's bowed, unkempt head. "She been a poor year for you, Bill?"

Bill shook his head and swallowed a bolted mouthful. "No, I've got plews, boys." he looked at them both with an ingratiating smile. "Was figuring I'd make a swap o' sorts with you if you'd pack 'em out for me and fetch back the gold come the spring rendezvous."

Seth snorted and Bill looked quickly over at him with a defensive, slightly aggrieved look. Seth's glance was half-smiling when he spoke: "You're a damned Big Belly for sure, Bill. You know we've got to haul out our take on our backs this year."

"Aw?" Bill said, without much conviction to the sound. "Where're your horses, boys? Injuns stole 'em?"

"Well," Seth said dryly, "they left us somehow. It's a safe guess Injuns got 'em, but we don't know it."

Bill made a clucking sound and heaped his wooden platter with more meat while doing it. "Well, 'course I been up on the Yellowstone an'—"

Seth snorted again. "Your horse is in the shed, isn't it, Bill?"

"Shore. Put 'im up afore I comed in."

"You didn't see any horse sign, did you?"

But Bill had known that was coming. He made an open-palm gesture of vast ignorance. "Dark out, Seth boy. A hungry man ain't alert an' you know that for a fact."

Jules threw back his head and laughed. Bill Williams shot him a darting look with amusement in it, then went back to eating. Jules's twinkling glance went to Seth. He winked merrily.

"Bill; how many pelts you got?"

"Not many," Bill said whiningly, knowing how Jules's mind was running. "You could carry 'em easy an' it'll be worth your time, Jules. Hear me, boys; I'm a little stiffed in the joints this fall. You'd help an old pardner, I know—that's why I comed in—that, an'—"

"Buffalo hump steaks," Seth said dryly, grinning tightly up around the eyes and letting the smell of his kinnikinnick tobacco flavour the cabin's warm, stuffy atmosphere.

Both Jules and Seth laughed that time. Old Bill's face lighted up briefly as he fished around for his pipe and flint and steel to light it with. He was finally full, having eaten more than Jules and Seth had together. Expansively he smiled at them both. He was absolutely beyond being insulted or angered now. The meat had been juicy and heavily fried in its ample grease. He puffed away thoughtfully for a while. No one spoke. It was a benign moment when all the peril and hardship was excluded. A mellow-

11

ness seeped into the atmosphere before Bill spoke again. He was looking drowsily into the fire.

"Run onto a bunch of Blackfeet bucks headin' for the Musselshell while I was on the trail. They was painted an' loaded for bear. Had a brace of whites with 'em, though. I give 'em a wide berth, cached and watched 'em make a camp." Bill's small, never-still eyes lifted to Seth's face. "First time I ever seen 'em take a white man prisoner. Hear me, boys, he was white: I seen him." The ferret-like eyes caught Seth's still, steady gaze. Bill stopped and looked at Jules too. Saw the same strange look, and shrugged.

"I don't blame you, boys. Only I ain't lyin', s'help me God. The other'n they had was a female white woman, an' that's a fact. A female white woman an' a growed white man."

"What'd you do?" Seth asked quietly.

Bill looked up quickly. "Do? Why, I just told you. I cached in the brush an' waited for 'em to filter on by, then I watched 'em make a camp, made certain they wasn't comin' back over their same trail, an' got to hell away from there. Come on down here to see you boys an' get you to pack—"

"Your furs out for you. All right. How long ago did you see 'em, Bill?"

"The Blackfeet? Yesterday. They was noonin' there on the Musselshell."

Seth knocked the dottle out into his palm and tossed it into the fireplace, then he looked over at Jules. The older man was regarding him steadily, silently, but with a knowing look on his face. The silence lingered until after Seth had put away his pipe and resurrected the little oval painting with its delicate hues and held it out towards Bill Williams. No words passed among them as Old Bill took the image and gazed at it critically.

"That's the female all right, Seth. You know her?"

"No. I found that where some Blackfeet'd hit a mule train of immigrants. That and some dead men."

"Sure," Bill said matter-of-factly. "Well, that's her all right, only her hair ain't done up like that now." He passed back the little painting and watched Seth pouch it, then swung his head and gazed at Jules. "I seen them mules. Wondered then, where they had thieved 'em. Big American mules—none of them Spanish jackasses, Jules. Make a man's mouth water to see 'em."

But Jules hadn't taken his eyes off Seth's face. He was sitting on a wall bench with his legs pushed far out and his work-hardened hands lying like dead things in his lap.

Bill Williams straightened a little and glanced from one to the other of them with a sniffing look. "What in tarnation's botherin' you two, boys? Them mules? Fergit it. That's a pretty powerful war band. You'd lose your hair certain a-creepin' up to steal mules off'n 'em."

"It's the girl," Seth said harshly. "She was alive yesterday at noon." He was looking past Bill at Jules. "She might still be alive."

Jules's chest heaved with a soundless sigh. Slowly, very slowly, he looked down at Bill Williams. There was that in his glance that was accusation and disgust both, but he said nothing. Bill Williams, however, was fast assuming an appearance of understanding. He, too, held the silence for a while, then very slowly and ponderously began to wag his shocklehead back and forth.

"You'd never git 'er done, boys. Never—as long as you live. You know how them fighting bucks look on something like that. A prize. A big prize. Live captives ain't often took. I been wonderin' ever since why they took the man. The girl—well—that's different. But you'd never get 'em, boys, an' that's a gut. Just noways would you ever get 'em."

Jules's glance at Old Bill was still unfriendly looking, but he kept his peace. Seth crossed the room closer to the fire and squatted. He was wearing fringed buckskins that

13

had been freshly washed. They were lighter by shades than the buckskins of his companions, from frequent washings in the cold, tumbling streams of the beaver creeks.

"Can't just leave her, though, Bill," Seth said solemnly, knowing even when he said it that Bill wouldn't agree. Knowing that Bill Williams's code didn't include a lot of things other men held to, including risking your topknot over a tomfool immigrant girl. Why worry about any member of the bands who were just beginning to tramp westward over the mountain men's domain!

Bill looked wryly at the younger man with a long and steady—and significantly cold—look. "Yes, you can, Seth, and you'll be wise to, let me tell you. Blackfeet're hard, boy. Damned few of us they like an' even them as they do don't live too long in their country. You know that like I do. You get to messin' around with 'em, you'll wind up hairless in a wash somewhere with your tendons all cut crossways." Bill looked over at Jules. "You tell him, Jules."

Jules pushed up a little on the hard bench and eased his weight to one side a little. "I don't know," he said, vaguely, evasively, with an odd look in his eyes. A faraway, secretive look Seth had never seen in his eyes before.

Bill snorted. "The hell you don't, you old buffalo gut. You've been in here a long time. I hear you an' Old Gabe pioneered these hills. You damned well know your Siksika."

Jules flashed an irate, impatient glance at Bill Williams. "Yes," he said with spirit, "an' I was here afore you come too. *An'* I'll be here after you're gone. But I ain't always been old an' out here neither. I can recall back to years when I was like Seth, if you can't. Now shut up!"

Bill, dumbfounded, looked from one to the other of them. Very slowly vast disgust spread over his hatchet features, then, with an animal growl that was part grunt, he rolled over on the buffalo robe nearest to him, grasped the edge in his hand and continued to roll until he was

14

wound tightly with only his head sticking out of the long cocoon. One more roll and his back was to them both, and to the fire also. Bill Williams, mountain man, was retiring.

Jules eyed the bundle of man and shaggy hide caustically. Bill had arbitrarily appropriated Jules's sleeping robe. Seth got up and banked the fire, pushed in a massive, wet length of wood and arose wiping the bark off his hands. He smiled wryly at Jules and motioned toward his own robe.

"Take it. I'll fetch one out of the bales."

When Seth was flattening out another fur, Jules looked over at him. "Well, what've you decided?"

"About the girl?"

Jules's face went swiftly irate, then cleared just as rapidly. "Yes," he said. "The girl."

"Why, I reckon I'll go after her in the morning."

Jules said no more. He lay down, felt for the robe's edge and rolled up with his eyes on Bill Williams's back. There was a dangerous dark flash to them, but Williams slept on as innocently as a babe.

Rolled up, Seth cleared his throat and spat into the fireplace. It made an angry, sizzling sound. "Jules? If they were going west after they killed the immigrants, and if Bill saw 'em on the Musselshell—where'd you reckon they're headed?"

The answer came back tired and muffled. "I'd reckon on 'em to be Bloods. Guess 'em to be makin' for Snow Mountain. They daren't go west too far or they'll be over in Flathead country. No, they'll cut north and more than likely make for Snow Mountain."

Unexpectedly Bill Williams's reedy twang came out of the buffalo robe cocoon. "You'd be right, Jules. They warn't Piegans or regular Siksika. They'd cut upland through them little hills afore Snow Mountain. There's a big camp of 'em up there. Seen it myself early this spring."

Seth lay back with his gaze on the powerful, barkless

15

tree trunks overhead that were the beams to hold up the sod roof. "That's a long way from here," he said musingly.

"Longer'n you know," Bill said with heavy meaning. "Be the longest trip you ever took, boy, mark my word."

Jules's answer came slower, more thoughtfully. "Bad time, Seth. The Big Sleep's about here. A man could freeze to death easy makin' that trip. Four feet of snow'd stop you cold an' leave you right there."

"I'll stay to the willow banks and trees," Seth said.

Jules had heard all he had to hear. He'd known it was coming anyway. But Bill Williams's robe quivered instantly with astonishment and his shrill, unpleasant voice came piercingly, like a bull elk's whistle, into the roomful of flickering, red-orange shadows that were growing larger as the fire died to a smoulder.

"You're goin' up there, Seth? Are you crazy, man? First off, the winter'll crack your bones an' freeze the marrow. Second place, you'll get scalped sure as God made grass. Third place—you darned fool—you'll never get to see th' girl. They'll split your head clean to the chin an' stuff it with rocks an' sink it in a creek. An' besides all that, they'll kill the girl long afore you'll ever git there. An' if they don't—mind me, Seth—you a-showin' up an actin' interested in her will make 'em rip her open like a gutted snowbird. They do that to prisoners first, when they figure folks are after 'em. Dang it; you know all that, Seth. Are you daft?"

"You forgot something," Seth's dry voice said. "I'll be snowed in if I reach them and don't get killed first, and that'll be about as bad as not reaching them."

Bill Williams struggled in his robe trying to crane his head around for a look, but had to give it up. He lowered his head with a wheezing groan. "Jules? You hear him? He's went crazy."

Jules growled some profanity that was thick with voyageur French, some Shoshoni and Blackfeet and Crow words, and the mcst select words among definitive—and

16

colourful—mountain man English, then he broke it off. "You are a damned gossip, Bill. Why didn't you just keep your trap shut about them prisoners?"

"How was I to know?" Bill whined.

"Well," Jules said pointedly, "you know now, an' you know what you've went an' stirred up for my old bones with winter a-comin' on—blast your beggin' old bones. So the least you can do, Bill Williams, is come along with us."

"Me?" Williams croaked in completely horrified astonishment. "Me? Gawd, Jules, you're daft too. I got a nice fat winter-warm squaw a-waitin' for me back up a ways anyway. 'Sides, you'll be walkin' to your own funerals. It's crazy, boys—you'll get killed afore you even see Snow Mountain."

"You brought the news, damn you," Jules persisted grimly.

"But I didn't know how it was, Jules. Naw—you're wilder'n a ruttin' pair of bulls if you think I'm goin' up there to lose my topknot over a immigrant female, boys. No sirree; not ol' Bill Williams. I'm goin' to fort up for the winter an' fetch in hides for a new suit an' eat real female cookin' an' get on some tallow." He lay back down and sniffled, cleared his throat, and spat. "I'll be at Pierre's Hole for the spring rendezvous, though. I'll search you out then, boys."

Seth had gone down to the creek to clean himself before they ate, a trait much admired by both old Jules and Bill Williams, but rarely emulated. Bill ran a grimy hand with ingrained dirt in the pores, like pigment itself, through his shocklehead and, staring mildly at Jules, spoke in his nasal, unpleasant voice.

"What'n thunderation's got into the man, Jules? They'll draw'n quarter him and feed his guts to their dogs. Blackfeet ain't Dakotas you can talk your way past with a lot of chest thumpin'. An' what's the girl to him?" Bill went over and ruminating with his tongue several times, spat into the newly fed fire, shaking his head all the while with the little weasel eyes darting, probing, never still, and suspicious.

"Seth's been away from the towns for three years, you understand, Bill. There's been squaws—but this one's white an' young and then there's that painted picture of her. I told him they never look like them pictures. Well," Jules shrugged eloquently, "the picture's hit him hard, Bill, so he's goin' after her."

Bill snorted again, softly that time, and peered closely at Jules. "Craziest damned thing I ever heard of, Jules. Tomfool crazy. They'll make an eagle whistle out of his skull-front and rattles out of his backbone." Bill looked around Jules at the frying meat in the skillet when next he spoke. "I see now why you were upset over me tellin' about them damn fool captives, but I didn't know, Jules, or I'd have kept still." He pointed with one long finger. "She's a-goin' to burn a little on the nigh side, Jules."

Jules turned his head, gazed at the frying meat with a soft grin tugging at the outer corners of his mouth—but sombre-eyed—and looked back at Bill Williams again. "It's all right. How many was in the war party, Bill?"

"Appeared to be about sixteen, eighteen. All painted up and marked for blood, too."

"You think they were headin' for Snow Mountain?"

"I'd reckon so. Leastwise they'd have to cut north an' there was a big Blood village up there early this spring, Jules. But—you'll never know where the red-hided sons are. They're worse than antelope for scuttlin' here an' there with their damned bitin' dogs an' stinking noise. Times a danged bird of some kind lights in a tree over a camp of 'em, an' they figure it's some kind of bad medicine. Down come the lodges, in come the ponies, on go the travois and away they go, spillin' all over the danged place, a-squawkin', cussin', screechin', and stirrin' up all the game critters an' a big dust. You know how it is with 'em, Jules."

But Jules was back by the skillet, screwing up his leathery face against the heat and flipping over the meat with his knife. Bill eased down cross-legged by the table and leaned his elbows on it with his bony face cupped in his hands. The little eyes flicked over the baled furs and a thought struck Bill.

"Jules, how'll you get all the furs out without Seth to help you?"

"Won't take 'em," Jules said succinctly, taking the meat out and sliding it onto the battered tins.

"Cache 'em here?" Bill asked calmly enough, then he caught the implication behind the words and he lifted his head, fixed Jules with the pale, baleful, suspicious little eyes and very slowly a look of disbelief spread over his features. "Jules, you're not," he said. "You're not goin' with this crazy danged fool?"

"I reckon I will," Jules said, still avoiding Bill's glance and carelessly shoving the tins about where the men would squat to eat.

Bill Williams sat up as straight as his perpetual stoop would allow, and exhaled a long, thin, rasping sound that could have been a sigh but wasn't. Then he broke into sound. "You're an idiot, Jules. A danged, mother's son of an idiot. Why—why—" but Bill couldn't put it all into words. Old Jules of all people to do such a suicidal thing. He looked stricken for a moment, then relaxed back into his hunched over posture and glared at the other man. Was still glaring at him in monumental, speechless, over-powering disgust when Seth came back into the cabin, went to the table and dropped down with a quick, tight smile at the other two. Not until then did Bill Williams take his gaze off Jules, look over accusingly at the younger man, and finally look down at his food.

"I'll cache my furs," he said to himself, "an' take 'em down to Pierre's Hole in the spring an' trade 'em off. Of

19

all the ridiculous things I ever heard this is the worst. Hear me now, boys—we're eatin' together for the last time. I tell you that right damned now. For the last time; mark me now. Now I ain't goin' to say another danged word to you about it."

Seth looked quickly and sharply at old Jules. "You'd better head out, Jules," he said quietly. "No sense in waiting for me."

"I'll foller along," Jules said, just as quietly, and ate as unconcernedly as though it was really nothing at all. No more, no less, than wading the icy creeks and setting traps, then wading them again to fetch the drowned beaver.

Seth looked at Jules a while with a soft scowl and finally went back to eating. He hadn't counted on that. Didn't exactly know whether he was pleased or not. A lone traveller could hide a lot of track. Two travellers—well, it was a heap harder to keep Injuns from picking up sign. Bill, having finished eating, wiped his knife on his pants leg and made the soft clucking sound of a wild hen turkey calling her young, indicating he was going to leave.

"Mind what I say, you two," Bill said, arising, unwinding his six-foot-two-inch frame. Its bare minimum of sinew and hide covered it so that he resembled a grotesque gargoyle dressed in soiled, ancient buckskin with most of the fringe used off the seams. "You're dead men, but if you wasn't—an' if you see the female—how do you plan to fetch her away from the Bloods?" He wagged his head dolorously and made a bitter face. "You'll never get her back. You know what you'll be doin'? Well—if she's still alive an' unspoilt when you git to her—*if* you do, which you won't—well, even then all you'll be doin' is makin' certain the Injuns split her head like a gourd. They allus do that when they suspicion whites're out to rescue their captives. Jules knows that, an' you ought to, Seth. You been trappin' with the free-trappers for five years now. That's a lifetime out here, boy. Now you're pushin' your luck too far. It's shame enough to see you go, Seth,

20

but you've got no right to take ol' Jules too. 'Tain't decent, Seth."

Seth got up, and carting his tin plate to the fireplace scraped the offal into the flames. "That's up to Jules, Bill. I think he ought to go out, but it's up t'him."

Jules finished eating and smiled at Bill. A rueful sort of smile, but determined. "I'll trail along with him, Bill. Used to know some Bloods, years back. Anyway, I can talk their lingo a little and Seth's lost there."

Bill looked from one to the other once more before he clapped his badger-fur hat on, crossed the room with a shambling, strangely sidling gait, picked up his rifle and hefted it. "All right, boys, you've heard me an' you're still dead set. All right. I'll go down to Pierre's Hole come spring rendezvous an' pass on where you went an' what's sure to happen to you. Goodbye to you an' good luck."

He didn't wait for an answer, but turned on his moccasined feet and, stooping low at the doorway, turned to his right and was gone. There was a quick sense of loss in the cabin, in spite of his garrulousness and whining tones, for old Bill Williams was one of the extremely rare mountain men who could go anywhere, alone, and always be counted upon to turn up alive again. One of the greatest members of that half-man, half-savage fraternity of free-trappers.

Jules chuckled. "Bill'll make it good, too, if we don't show up at rendezvous."

"Yep," Seth said. "He'll make it good either way. If we do or if we don't." He looked over at Jules. "Why don't you head out? This is a crazy idea of mine, Jules. No sense in you riskin' your hair-lock too."

"No," Jules said, "no sense to it, boy. But I been without sense so long now losin' a mite more won't harm me. As for my topknot, she's pretty thin on top. I don't think they'd take it anyway." He was smiling with that firm, unyielding way he had. Seth saw it, understood it, and desisted. They would go together then.

CHAPTER TWO

IT was a big country. From the Yellowstone north-west-ward there were serrated little humps that were the hills along the living river; beyond the little hills was a prairie of sorts, with knobs scattered across it here and there, like the mud hovels of desert tribesmen, then the land began to lift a little. Rise up again with more serrated humps of land. Beyond those was the Musselshell river. Seth and Jules made their way cautiously. Especially across the open meadows and random prairies.

On the Musselshell they quartered. It was Jules that found the old camp described by Bill Williams. He waited by it, hunkered and thoughtful, until Seth came up, then he pointed at the signs on the earth.

"Never did figger ol' Bill could count. Warn't more'n fifteen o' 'em."

Seth squatted saying nothing, reading the impressions and correcting his own earlier estimate downwards, then he nodded. "You're right." He bent a little, picked up a twig and raked gravely at the blackness where the cooking fire had been. Something curled and withered showed among the ashes. It was a moccasin that had been water soaked and badly torn before being discarded. Seth took it up and worked the leather. He smoothed it out enough for them both to see the ragged beaded symbol of a three-pronged object that resembled a hay-fork. Yet it was nothing so peaceful in intent. It was the tribal sign of the Blackfeet—the Siksika, as they called themselves—indicating the three divisions of the tribal confederacy. The Piegans, the Siksika proper, and the Bloods.

Jules grunted. "Nothin' we didn't know," he said.

Seth tossed the moccasin aside and felt for the little parfleche sack at his belt, tugged aside the drawstrings and began to eat pemmican with slow, rhythmic movements of his jaws. His glance swept easily and far-ranging over the more or less open, broken land north of them.

"Not far now, Jules."

The older man ate with identical aplomb. "No," he agreed, "but from now it'll be worse. We've got t'watch double, boy. They'll have hunters out. Maybe war parties too, but she's mighty cold for that kind o' business—an' late in th' year."

"And what if they aren't there any more?" Seth's gaze was resting on the tumble of rock and wilderness that lay across their path.

Jules shrugged a little. He didn't actually care whether they were or weren't. What worried him more than anything else was the gradual build-up overhead. The immense vacuum of silence and unreasonable warmth, and slate-greyness that meant a big blizzard was building up. Death in the snow was a familiar spectre to all of them. Every trapper lived with it constantly, and because of the never dormant fear of it, they were careful. Jules rocked back a little and gazed at the opaque sky. He said nothing.

Seth got up and waited for Jules, then they started out again, but now their trail couldn't be direct and forward. There was far too much open country. Travelling westward along the river, using the willows and gnarled brush as covert, they made fairly good time. Seth's mind was planning ahead as he twisted and turned, brushed aside the clawing, spiny fingers of brush and limbs. If they were caught by Blackfoot hunters and taken back prisoners, or killed outright, they would soon be forgotten. They had to approach the village under their own power and prove their ability to the Indians by coming down among them unsuspected.

The Blackfeet were no different from any other Plains Indians. They respected courage and would be greatly impressed by any whites who could enter their very village without being seen first. Moreover, the fate of a captive was certain. The fate of guests depended largely upon themselves, for the Blackfeet, unlike the Dakotas, weren't a grim, haughty people. They laughed freely and loved dignity, but they also were a sensible people, unless riled.

Seth went forward knowing all this and determining to use each segment of the whole to their best advantage, if he could. He kept to the game trails westward until he came to a wide, much travelled old buffalo trace, then stopped to get his bearings. Jules came up silently beside him and motioned with his arm at the wide, dusty trail.

"Buffalo road. They use it goin' an' comin' from the Teton Basin. There's salt-grass and grazin' below Fort McKenzie, in that upper country."

Seth nodded. "I reckon," he said. "Seems to me it winds right up through the Belts and comes out onto the plain over by the Great Falls."

"Aye." Jules said with a brusque nod. "It does. Now, if you keep north into the Belts we'll have plenty o' cover, for there's a heap of mountains around us now."

Orientated, Seth gazed steadily at the upthrusts around them and ahead. "We trapped up here the first year I came out, Jules," he said. Then he turned and gazed at the older man. Jules's face was pinched with the cold, ruddy and weathered looking. His dark eyes were pinpoints behind the overhangs of flesh that were his perpetual squint, and the eyes themselves were never still. They probed everywhere, always moving, like the eyes of a wild animal. "I reckon we'd do best to hold north until we're behind Snow Mountain, then come down south again. Seems to me that's the best route for cover."

Jules nodded and jutted his chin toward a wide, much trampled spot where some whitish crystals clung to the base rocks. "Salt," he said matter-of-factly. "I expect we could count a coup here if we wanted to squat an' wait.

24

Plenty of buffalo sign. Injuns must know about that salt-lick too."

Seth followed Jules's glance and saw the white exudations. He went over and broke off several and saw where the larger deposits had been worn as smooth as glass from the generations of buffalo tongues that had licked them. Jules came up and broke off several pieces too. They pouched some and put smaller pieces into their mouths and started off again.

Night caught them in the erosion gullies of the Belt Mountains. A land of rolling rock and earth where brush and grass grew almost as tall as a man. The cold was like a knife. Even sleeping robes wouldn't keep it out. They ate in stony silence, rolled up and lay there, each with his thoughts. Jules looked sombrely at the swollen-looking heavens and had grave misgivings. Seth considered their position and undertaking objectively, and for the first time was beset with serious doubts about his wisdom.

By morning, though, both knew they would have to move fast and keep right on moving, for it was snowing. Being caught in the hills if the snow turned into a blizzard would be fatal. They broke camp and trudged on again, their smoke-tanned moccasins turning the dampness a little, but not the cold. Hurrying forward until the constant climbing and slipping and exertion made the sounds of their hearts beat loudly in their ears.

Seth fought his way to a goodly hill and stood hunched against a bitter, slicing wind that scourged the spot. He heard Jules grunt and swung his head to look behind them. There, in the faint distance was the clearly definable outline of Hell-Gate, so named because the Flathead buffalo hunters and war parties came boiling down into the Blackfoot country through its granite passes, fanned out and carried terror over the southern countries. He looked around again. Gazed for a long time at a distant jagged spire that was Snow Mountain, then touched Jules's arm with his hand and pointed. Smoke. They both shivered and looked. Spirals of smoke rising as straight up as the flight of an arrow. Up until it looked to Seth as though it must flatten out against the lowering belly of the sky. Smoke fingers; not just a few either. He turned to Jules.

"That must be the village."

Jules nodded, saying nothing. His hawkish profile was drawn down like a drum-head. It made him look twenty years younger. Seth nudged him again and chopped downward with his chin, Indian fashion, pointing.

"Hunters."

There, about a half mile below and south of them, were four horsemen riding slowly, bunched over into the face of the snow, which was increasing in intensity so that, by the time Seth looked up again, toward the distant village, it was lost in the obscurity of the myriad flakes.

Jules spoke into the wind that tore at them. His words were whipped away over his shoulder. "They got something. Maybe an antelope. Blackfeet all right. Going back to the village now." He glanced at the sky and dropped his gaze to Seth's face. It was impassive. "I don't know whether we're lucky or unlucky. We see a village when we've got to cache—that's luck." He didn't say any more. Just broke it off like that and gazed at the closed-in distances where the Blackfoot village lay.

He didn't have to say any more. Seth understood. He started down off the mountain without glancing at Jules. The snow was wet and treacherous. His footing was never safe but he broke over into a little jog and held to it until he was back down among the marshy lowlands where the gullies were easily avoided. There, he waited a moment for Jules, then struck out due south. Held that course until some instinct made him alter it a little. Then he went east a few degrees and stayed on the new course until the land began to slope downward, as though sliding toward some distant rise, and then he stopped and squatted in the snow-bent reeds and watched Jules come in and hunker.

Jules ate his pemmican without speaking, casting suspicious glances overhead every once in a while. Seth, seeing, did likewise. The sky had an odd bloatedness to it. It appeared low enough so that Seth might reach up and touch it. For the first time he fully understood Jules's uneasiness.

"Blizzard, Jules."

"I reckon," the older man said laconically. "Seen it like this once before, long time back. Snowed so's it nigh covered the Injuns' tipis." He shrugged. "But you can't tell. Might come wind an' blow it all away." An irrelevant thought struck old Jules and he smiled at it. "Bill'll stay put an' warm this winter."

Seth finished eating, got up carefully and flexed his legs; the cold was penetrating and congealing. West of them would be about where they'd seen the Blackfoot hunters. He waited for Jules, then swung his arm in a stiff arc. "Over there somewhere we could cut the sign of those hunters." he made no move though.

Jules tightened the pucker-string of his parfleche pouch and shook his head. "Might find somethin' else too, if that's a trace they use often."

"Yeh." Seth turned and without another word or glance at old Jules, swung into his sloppy little jog and went through the reeds and over the snow again, south and a little eastward.

The snow was intensely cold by the time he stopped. The flakes were as large as silver dollars, coming down steadily, lazily, and with a frightful silence that made Seth more uneasy than ever. He swore under his breath. Visibility was limited to not more than twenty feet ahead. He turned and watched Jules's shadowy form emerge out of the whiteness.

"Jules. My figuring says we're damned close. You smell anything?"

Jules shook his head wryly. "Be pretty hard to do, now boy." The older man's cheeks were burnished reddish copper colour and his dark eyes were restless under the hoar-frost on his shaggy eyebrows. "Where you reckon that village is from here?"

"Not more than a half mile ahead." Seth's gaze dropped to Jules's rifle, saw the dampness of it and frowned. "Well, we got this far," he said dubiously. "Let's get on."

They did. Walking with increasing difficulty as the snow-banks dragged at their moccasined feet. Floundering occasionally and cursing. Then Seth saw the shaggy, head-down, humped backed figures ahead of them and froze where he was. It took several seconds to identify the objects. He turned his head to Jules. "Horses. We're pretty close."

Jules nodded and jutted his chin. Seth moved closer to the animals, knowing their chance of smelling the white men was very remote under the circumstances. He and Jules hunkered behind a dense copse of snow laden chap-parral and studied the herd. It appeared to be large. As far as they could make out, anyhow, there were horses beyond those closest to them, like black wraiths struck motionless by the silky snowflakes. He turned to Jules and made the motion for "sit-wait." One fist thrown shoulder high, then jerked down vertically, abruptly, and held there a second. Jules nodded, not comprehending what Seth had in mind, but not worrying either.

Seth moved out toward the nearest horse. The animal didn't throw its head up until he was quite close, then it snorted and came erect, little ears forward and eyes wide with curiosity. Seth felt for one of the chunks of salt he'd taken back at the salt-lick, palmed it, held it out before him. The animal's wariness was divided between fear and wonder. He didn't move, but neither did Seth, knowing one quick gesture on his part would frighten not only the horse in front of him, but all the Blackfoot horses.

He stood until his arm ached. The horse bobbed its head a couple of times, then the curiosity won out. He lowered his muzzle and sniffed sceptically. Seth waited

28

with his teeth locked against the paralysing cold. Another, closer sniff, and the horse caught scent of the salt and came closer. After that it was easy. Seth let him lick the stuff and finally gave it to him. He used his belt to catch the animal. The second animal was easier to catch. He led them both back to Jules and grinned through blue lips. Jules got up stiffly and smiled back at him.

"We're close enough to ride right in among 'em, Jules. Come on."

The old trapper hoisted himself aboard with effort, then shook his head ruefully. "They might laugh at it, at that, Seth," he said. Seth held the single rein of his improvised war-bridle, gazing over the horse herd. If the village was beyond, he couldn't see it. He reined around anyway, and kneed the horse out around the herd, southward.

They hadn't ridden more than twenty minutes before they saw the first lodge. It was a conical thing that seemed to jump up out of the snow directly in their path. There was a gusty spiraling of smoke coming out of the snow-laden circle of lodgepoles overhead. Seth turned and made a sign to Jules. They rode past that first lodge and continued southward some little distance until they came upon more lodges.

Then, they were in the village.

Once, a dog barked at their passing, but otherwise the camp was still and silent. Grinning triumphantly, Seth led them until they came to the centre of the village, and there, according to the custom of the Blackfeet, was the large, impressive, circle of headsmen's lodges with the little space all around them that separated the tipis of the leaders from the other lodges. Seth reined up his Blackfoot horse, twisted and gazed at old Jules. The old trapper's face was wreathed in a wide grin. Whatever came now, at least they had completely surprised the wary Blackfeet, and that was, in the eyes of any mountain man or Indian, quite a feat.

Seth swung down, lifted one water-logged moccasin and worked it in a little circle pivoting on his ankle, then lowered that foot and repeated the manœuvre with his other foot. The circulation wasn't completely restored, but it was stimulated. He turned and watched Jules dismount, leave his horse and walk over. Seth shrugged, touched his thoroughly damp rifle and made the quick, flitting gesture for being helpless, then shrugged again, tapped the tomahawk in his belt and went forward.

By squinting overhead, studying the lodgepoles where they stuck up above the hides that covered their extremities, Seth was able to determine the lodge in front of them had twenty-six poles. It would be the tipi of a leader. He went over by the door-flap, cast another glance at Jules, saw the intentness in his friend's eyes, lifted the flap and entered.

Immediately a wall of warmth struck him. There was a fierce-burning fire in the centre of the lodge, in the fire-hole, and the smoke went straight up. There were Indians in there too. The head of the family, straight ahead of Seth, across the fire, staring at him with unblinking, black-eyed regard and wooden impassiveness, and two boys on his left, the older boy next to the warrior, the youngest boy farther away. To the Blackfoot's right were two young girls, arranged like the sons, so that the oldest girl was next to her father, the youngest beside the older girl. And behind the buck, as though welded to the ground and unable to move, her head cast around slightly over one shoulder, black eyes staring at Seth, was the squaw.

Seth waited until Jules was inside, batting his eyes against the brilliance of the fire and the benevolent warmth, then he moved abruptly toward the Blackfoot warrior, going to the right of the fire-hole, around past the frightened but blank-faced girls, and stopping near the warrior. The Blackfoot got up very slowly. He was as tall as Seth and warmly dressed in buckskin with a trade-blanket belted at the middle. He didn't speak. In fact, no one did, although the squaw's mouth was open a little, as though she might.

The buck then gestured for his oldest son to give way a little. The lad did. His movement seemed to break a spell. The others of the man's family turned their heads from Jules near the door-flap, to younger, more erect Seth. The host then motioned Seth to the vacated place on his left. They both sat down. Jules watched the ceremony of seating a guest with vast inner amusement, for he knew —as did everyone else in the big lodge—that the emergence of two strange white men out of the night, right in the very heart of a Blackfoot village, had all but petrified the Indians with astonishment.

The Blackfoot, seeing Jules wasn't going to come around and be seated, nodded at him. Those who had something to say when they entered a Blackfoot lodge, held to their place at the door-flap until given permission to speak. The big buck nodded twice before Jules spoke.

"We come in peace among the Siksika," Jules said in the throaty, gusty tongue of the Blackfeet. "We return the strayed horses of my brother." Jules rocked his head backwards a little, indicating the out-of-doors. "The horses are there." He stood perfectly motionless, giving stare for stare with the big Indian.

The silence grew and grew. Seth was watching the Indian's face out of the corner of his eye. There was nothing to see there, however. Just a flinty hardness mixed with owlish wariness. The Blackfoot was clearly caught off balance by two such startling apparitions. After a dignified interval of silence, he spoke very gravely—and Seth sighed inwardly.

"The Bloods welcome guests—even white ones. They thank their white brothers for bringing back strayed Blood horses." He paused a moment, studying Jules's face with the same close intensity he had first directed against Seth. "I am glad you came in peace," he said simply.

Then Jules smiled. It was an ironic, mocking little smile

31

and the Blackfoot didn't miss interpreting it as such. He looked away from Jules and swung his glance to Seth, held it there a long moment, then very slowly stood up to his full height and motioned Jules to the place on his left beside Seth.

"You are wet. You are hungry. You will be fed and cared for. I go."

They both watched him leave the tipi. Neither white man doubted for a second where he was going nor that he would fail to inform the rest of the village of their abrupt materialisation out of the lowering dusk. Then they ate. The squaw, her lips pulled flat against her teeth and avoiding their glances, fed them from the little iron pot.

Once, Seth glanced around at Jules. The old trapper was grinning to himself as though at some huge joke. Seth finished eating and gazed frankly at the two girls across from him. They were young, probably in their early teens. He looked at the sons of the Blackfoot. They were even younger. The squaw looked to be in her late thirties. She was a handsome, tall woman with features thinner, less mongoloid, than other Plains Indians Seth had come to know since becoming a free-trapper. She caught his glance and returned it steadily. Apparently her earlier fright or startled anger, or whatever it was, had dissipated itself. He grinned a little, thinking back to the equal curiosity of the Blackfoot horse and wondering amusedly what the squaw's reaction would be if he offered her a pebble of salt, too.

Jules had finished eating. He smiled very gravely at the two boys beside him, who returned his nod with the same big-eyed stare they'd worn since the white men had first come into the lodge. Then Jules grinned. It made his worn, white teeth stand out in contrast to the steel-dust of his beard stubble. Grey-black with ivory white mixed in.

The look had the effect of heightening the terror of the

little girls. At least until the squaw begrudgingly broke the silence, ignoring the white men and speaking to the children. Then Jules laughed. It was a pleasant, homely sound. The squaw threw him a quick look. Seth was watching the awkward little drama with interest as he stoked up his Blackfoot pipe and lit it from the fire-hole.

Jules curbed his laughter but the grin lingered. His black eyes twinkled at the Blackfoot woman. "Let them stare. At least they aren't Crows to hide their heads under blankets."

The woman answered Jules waspishly. "They are strong-hearts," she said, "why should they fear? To stare is not good, though."

"Ah-h," Jules grunted. "They do not often see white men."

The squaw turned and flung a look of venom at Jules. Seth was surprised at its latent hatred. "If the Siksika had *never* seen white men it would have been better. That these children never see them would be better still."

Jules regarded the woman with good-natured silence, then he shrugged and turned fully to face Seth. "Well— you pieced together whose lodge we're in?"

Seth nodded slowly, ranging his glance from the buffalo-neck shield with its scars and marks of much use, to the symbols painted across it. To the coup stick and war-bonnet with the twin trailers of tufted eagle feathers, and to the very martial display of weapons—even including a long-rifle with a hickory stock. "I reckon, Jules. Seems his name's Plume. He belongs to the Horn society and is a first-class warrior."

"But we missed the chief's lodge," Jules said. Then, as though to console himself, he added. "It don't make no difference though. This un's a big pipe-smoker, anyway."

"We'll meet the chief soon enough," Seth said dryly. "You want to use that yarn you told Plume about the strayed horses?"

33

Jules's eyes twinkled. "That didn't fool the old buck much, boy. Not when he seen our leggings as wet as they are, and our moccasins soaked from a heap of walkin'. No; you've under-rated him, Seth."

"Then we'd better just say we got caught out in the storm an' came in to our brothers to get warm and wait it out."

Jules nodded slowly. "It's simple enough to be true," he said, then glanced around quickly when the Blackfoot appeared in the opening of his lodge, stared at them a moment, then beckoned.

"You come now," he said, and stepped aside as they both went back out into the snow. It was almost knee-deep. Jules pursed his lips and squinted at the sky. The warrior went around them, saw Jules's glance heavenward and grunted. "Medicine-storm," he said.

Jules followed in the buck's tracks speaking aside to Seth. "They call any big storm they didn't count on hittin' 'em a 'medicine-storm.' They figure it's somethin' special, you see; like—well—"

"Like we'd say 'God-sent.' I know."

Jules crooked his neck and gazed at Seth, then hurried ahead in the wake of the Blackfoot until they were before a large, much decorated tipi with pictographs running completely around it, telling of the innumerable coups counted by the householder. Plume held aside the door-flap. Seth ducked low and entered. Immediately he was conscious of many men around the fire-hole. Not one glanced up as they entered. He studied their faces frankly, until Jules and Plume were inside too, then the man up at the head of the circle of Blackfoot warriors lifted his head very slowly and gazed at the white men.

Seth was struck at once by the gravity and frankness of the dusky face. He held his glance to the Indian's, knowing that to allow one's gaze to waver before the stare of another—in Indiandom—was the surest preliminary indication of fear or cowardice. Staring, he heard the faint

34

rustle as the other Blackfeet also looked up at the white men, then Plume was speaking. Seth caught a word now and then. Enough to understand that Plume was again, officially this time, reciting the abrupt entrance of the strangers into his lodge. He kept his glance over the heads of the lesser warriors and fixed steadily on the face of the chief.

After what seemed a long interval of complete silence, the chieftain shifted his glance from Seth to Jules, and spoke. "I know you. You came among us long ago with Big Throat." (Meaning Jim Bridger. So-called by the plains tribesmen because of his goitre). Jules inclined his head once, then stood there, hip-shot, giving glance for glance and showing nothing but patience in his expression.

"Why do you come among us again?"

Jules motioned towards Seth. "My brother and I were hungry. We were caught by the medicine-storm. Our feet were guided to the village of our brothers the Siksika."

A low murmur ran among the assemblage. Seth wanted to smile at old Jules, but he didn't. Shrewdly, Jules had used the blizzard as though it was part of their arrival. The mysterious medicine-storm the Indians were uneasy about.

"You came alone? Just the two of you?"

"We did," Jules said.

"Who is he?" One chop of the square jaw in Seth's direction signified who the leader meant. Seth waited, wondering how Jules would name him.

"He is Medicine-Walker," Jules said without batting an eye. "A strong man of healing among the white men."

That brought their heads up for a long, probing stare at Seth. He felt uneasy under it. Several of the warriors grunted appreciation. "Hou; hou." The chief looked a little puzzled. His scowl was slight but unmistakable.

"The Medicine-Walkers of the white men are many this winter." Again his councilmen grunted approval and agreement. Jules, puzzled in turn, looked long and searchingly at the head man.

"How? Many? Medicine-Walkers are never many. They are a sacred brotherhood among all tribes."

"It is so," the chief said, "but we have another white medicine man too."

Seth's understanding broke over him in a wave. That was why they had saved the white man. Some way, they had either known or found out that he was a doctor. Always deeply respectful of strong medicine of any kind, the Blackfeet had taken him alive.

Jules was still groping though. Looking his perplexity, he spoke it when he took up the conversation once more. "How can this be? Is there a white medicine-man living among the Bloods?"

Some among the warriors smiled a little, glancing slyly up at Jules and Seth. The chief didn't smile though, when he answered. "No. He is a captive. He was taken alive in a raid."

Jules understood then and shot Seth a triumphant look before he nodded at the chieftain. "So be it. One medicine-man is your prisoner. The other is your guest, come among you with a good heart and a straight tongue."

Plume now stepped around them and stared gravely at the chief. Seth instantly caught the impulses of friction that came into the atmosphere. He watched Plume's thin, aquiline features, then turned and looked at the leader. As though some obscure veil had been dropped over his face, the expression had altered noticeably. There was a granite set to his jaw and a brutal cant to his mouth, otherwise his features were flinty and impassive. Seth grasped the feeling that there was some kind of deep and bitter animosity between the two warriors.

Plume, though, was an eloquent speaker. The longer he spoke, the less Seth liked either Plume, or his and Jules's chances of remaining free men. Holding out a muscular arm rigidly toward the white men, Plume thundered his denunciation. Here was no friend of white men, whether they came in peace or war.

"If the medicine-storm brought them, then it was another evil along with the deep snow. No good has ever come to the people from the white men. Not from the quick-killing-sickness [the smallpox epidemic of 1837-38 that killed over one half the Blackfoot tribe; over six thousand Siksika of all ages and both sexes] to the big-belly guns.

"Nothing has ever come from them but bad. We are their enemies. We fight them now and always should. My Sits-Beside-Me-Woman (his chief wife) lost her mother and three brothers when the traders at Fort McKenzie shot the cannons into them.

"These men stole among us. They cannot have come in friendship. They are white. They are our enemies. They have come to kill us in our sleep; to stampede our horses, to injure us greatly. It has always been this way. Big Throat made promises then left without fulfilling them. Since, he has armed the Snakes with white-man guns and they have killed our people. These men are our enemies. I have spoken."

The harangue had different results. Murmurs of "hou, hou," came from among the warriors in the circle. Plume lifted his glance and held it proudly over the heads of the seated men, meeting the glance of no man, but undoubtedly giving the reaction to his talk.

Seth looked boldly at the big warrior. That he was their foremost enemy so far, none would deny. The chief looked back toward Jules, waiting. Seth wanted to turn fully and coach his pardner but he didn't. Any show of interest was beneath a brave man. He was supposed to stand there reflecting polite interest and near-boredom. He did, but it was hard. Then Jules was speaking again, the words a soft slur that seemed to ameliorate the explosiveness of the language.

"My brother is a great warrior. A strong-heart. He is also a hater of white men. Among my people there are also haters of Red men. Somewhere between are the true white men and the true Red men. We are in this land together. We fight when we must. But we also live in peace together. My heart is good. Medicine-Walker's heart is good. We came in peace. Does my brother think two white men with wet powder would come among the Bloods in war? Then he needs a new vision for his medicine-thoughts are weak.

"I have lived among the Pikuni (Piegans). I have brothers among them. Send a runner and ask. I am called Beaver Killer among the Pikuni."

Instantly Plume, obeying Blackfoot etiquette, which forbade the interruption of anyone, even the most hated of enemies, spoke out again in his thundering, battlefield voice. Seth's dislike of the man became a seething fury in his chest. He tried to look indifferent but wasn't altogether successful at it.

"If these white men came among us in peace, as they say, why did they come among us at this time? Are our buffalo paunches so many that we can take in and feed those who stagger out of the medicine-storm? Why do they come like beggars in the night? To eat us weak so that in the spring other whites can make war against a weakened people?"

Seth's knowledge of Blackfoot was limited, but it was equal to his pithy answer. "My brothers," he said, haltingly, screwing up his face in the effort to form and mouth the difficult words. "We will hunt for our food. We will live in the snow if you cannot offer us a lodge. We would treat you differently if you came to our cabin in the winter, but if this is the custom of the Bloods, we will bow to it."

His answer to Plume's denunciation made several of the older Indians glance disapprovingly at Plume. One even covered his face with his turkey-wing fan, indicating that he was ashamed and didn't want to look upon a man who

38

had talked thus. The silence lasted only a moment, then the chieftain spoke again, looking at Plume as much as at the two white men.

"If these men come as friends, the Bloods are not Snakes to turn them away. If they come as enemies," he paused and looked long at Seth and Jules, "we will have a long winter to know them as such. We have little enough food, but we have a lodge for them. The one called Medicine-Walker can serve the people. In the time of Long Sleep there is always illness. Strong white man medicine can help our own medicine. We are not Crows to scoff at good medicine. We see strong-hearts among us. We will welcome them."

The other warriors within the council-circle made grunts of approval. Seth glanced once, swiftly and triumphantly, at Plume. The warrior would not meet his glance. He stared stonily over the heads of them all. A stalwart old fighting man with a tuft of hair gathered at the very top of his head and bound tightly so that it stuck up like a miniature tree, arose and held his blanket tightly to his big frame.

"I will take the white men to their lodge." He waited. No one offered further argument. Seth watched as the buck broke the circle, circled the cross-legged men respectfully and jerked his head at him and Jules.

Outside the storm was whistling and howling among the lodges. The hide walls bellied out then fell back slack, limning the lodgepoles beneath so that the effect was as if the tipis were great, conical beasts gaunt and bowed under the force of the blizzard.

The Blackfoot braced against the storm and fought his way through the drifts toward a lodge set a little apart from the others. It was an old, much patched tipi with faded, meaningless pictographs painted on its cracking covering. He worked at the flap and worried it open, stepped high over the snow-guard and stood to one side as the white men entered. The place was bitter cold and draughty. Jules went at once to the little supply of faggots by the fire-hole and went to work. Seth turned and regarded the Blackfoot's lined face and coal-black eyes for a moment, then he spoke.

"My brother helps those who need help. I will not forget."

The Blackfoot appeared to be about to say something, then he paused a moment longer, and when he did finally speak, the words were in English. "Man make heap trouble. Man make heap fight. Big storm make worse trouble. Man no can fight now. Man wait."

Seth nodded wryly. "You're damned right," he said in English. "Until the storm's over we'll just wait and see."

The Blackfoot nodded, catching the drift, then he went out. Seth turned to the anæmic little fire Jules had burning and squatted by it. "That's one thing we're all in agreement on, Jules. Until this storm's over none of us can do much for each other."

"Or *to* each other," Jules said. "You've made it, boy." The black eyes looked across the smudge of pungent smoke at Seth. "I reckon that's about a third o' what you've got in mind."

Seth smiled and crossed his legs under him and fished around for his stone pipe. "One thing, Jules. We've made old Bill Williams a liar. He said we wouldn't even get here."

Jules grunted and shoved his damp shanks toward the fire. "'Tain't hard to make a liar out of old Bill," he said dryly, "only, if the rest of it don't turn out right, no one'll be around to tell him he's one."

Seth smoked and watched the steam rise from his feet and legs. "They're alive and here, Jules."

"*He* is, you mean. Wonder how they knew he was a doctor?" Without awaiting an answer, which he didn't consider important anyway, Jules went on. "That Plume —dang good thing we barged right into his wickiup. If

40

he'd stumbled onto us outside, there'd have been a killin' fight, certain."

"Jules; did you see anything in that lodge that'd tell you the chief's name?"

"You weren't studyin', Seth. There was a medicine-shield hangin' over by the war bonnet. His name's Black Horse. He's a Kit-Fox warrior."

Seth smoked until his pipe went out, then he ate pemmican, thinking ahead. Neither of them spoke again until dawn awakened them with its terrible cold. The little fire was dead in the fire-hole.

CHAPTER THREE

SETH made a new fire and went out into the snow. It was three feet deep but had stopped falling during the night. He looked at the village. There was the smell of wood-smoke in the leaden air and his breath was thick and white looking. He noticed the tipi he and Jules shared was a good three hundred feet from the nearest lodge. A glance at the snow around them indicated that not too long before, Indians had made tracks around the place. He made a wry face, washed in the snow and went back inside. Jules looked up and grinned when he came up close to the fire and squatted.

"How many lodges?"

Seth shrugged. "Didn't count 'em, but it's a pretty big camp. Nice wintering spot too."

Jules was eating. "I know this spot," he said. "The Injun name means Moon Prairie. We trapped this over about six, eight years back. There's a little creek east of us. Over by them buttes. Injuns like to winter here for the willows along it. Keeps their horses alive in bad winters. You've never seen this spot in summer, I don't expect. Mighty pretty spot. Sort of land-locked valley. Pretty big too." Jules poked at the fire a little.

"You know, I reckon this is a birthin' tent. Blackfeet always have one around permanent camps. Set 'em up an' leave 'em a little ways off so's their babies can be borned in 'em."

Seth smiled thinly at Jules. "That," he said, "or the lodge of someone that's died. They abandon lodges folks die in, too."

42

Jules looked up quickly with a long, steady glance, but he said nothing for a while, then, when he did speak, he wasn't looking at Seth. "Why did you say that?"

Seth twisted where he sat and pointed to some dark maroon stains along the inner lining of the lodge, near the door-flap. "Blood over there. Probably came off some mourner."

Jules peered intently at the indicated spot. His small smile faded gradually. "Damn," he said, and that was all. Seth laughed at him. Jules shook his head back and forth very seriously. " 'Tain't nothin' to laugh at, boy. You know why they leave tipis folks die in?"

"I reckon," Seth said, still grinning. "Ghosts."

Jules fired a reproachful glance at his companion. "There's such things, Seth. I can tell you."

"Maybe. I don't know. I *do* know ghosts in here with us might be a help. We're not in any position to refuse any help. Even ghost-help."

"No," Jules said with a scowl, "you've no call to make light of 'em. Bad medicine, boy. Bad medicine."

Seth finished his pemmican breakfast and eyed the older man askance, but he said no more on the subject. If he didn't believe in spirits and old Jules did, it wasn't a difference that annoyed him. He'd been among the old fur trappers too long not to recognise that most of them— Jules included—were a strange mutation of Indian and white man. Their ideas had been borrowed largely from the savages, lacking white-man training in the things they later came up against. With one or two exceptions, the mountain men were vastly ignorant whites. Religion was nothing they knew about nor cared to know about. Thus, when they came up against the vast spirituality of the red men, they adopted a lot of the Indian beliefs. Jules was such a man. He evidenced it in his uneasiness for fear the lodge they inhabited was the deserted home of a departed Blackfoot.

43

Seth broke the awkward silence with an observation he'd made when he was outside. "They must've had a guard around us last night. Lots of tracks in the snow, Jules."

Back on familiar ground again, Jules spoke calmly enough. "I reckon," he said matter-of-factly. "They'll be watchin' us like hawks from now on. Plume's got the fightin' bunch stirred up against us by now. They'll be itchin' for a reason to stick an arrow in our backs. Well," he looked over at Seth and grinned with his eyes, "we got that a-comin', you know." He tugged up the string of his pouch and canted his head for a long look at the sky where it was visible up the smoke-hole. "Still snowin' out?"

"No. She's stopped, but it's colder'n a Dakota's heart and grey looking." Seth got up and let the fire's warmth fan out over the full length of his body. Back to the fire, he studied the little dried blood splashes on the inner tipi wall by the flap.

Blackfoot custom in mourning was for the aggrieved to mutilate themselves in their abandoned grief. Among the men this was carried out with ritualistic gravity and usually ended with a slash across the chest and the prescribed wailing. But among the women the forms of self-torture often included deep and serious slashing of the breasts, the chopping off of a finger or a portion of a finger and the days-long keening and bleeding and rending of garments.

Seth turned away from the stains and looked appraisingly at Jules. "Reckon I'll go hunt up those whites."

Jules got up and shook his head vigorously. "You'd better not, Seth. Bloods ain't fools, boy. They're suspicious of us already. Let 'em get a scent of the way the wind's a-blowin', an' they'll kill them prisoners so quick you'll never have a chance to get more'n a peek at 'em."

Seth stared into the little fire for a moment. "All right," he said. "I'll go talk to Black Horse and do a little scouting around."

"Handle it smart, boy," Jules cautioned him with a

steady, unblinking look. "They ain't idiots by a dang sight. Smarter than most Injuns an' don't forget it. Walk soft, Seth." He squatted by the fire again. "I'll wait here. See if you can borrow a brace of horses too, while you're out a-visitin'. We'll have to do some huntin' or eat pemmican till our fangs drop out."

Seth went out into the big drifts. Once, fleetingly, he caught a glimpse of a dark face peering at him from the closest lodge to his own. He didn't smile but the inclination was there. The Blackfeet, for all their known hospitality, were taking no chances. Acting as though he hadn't seen the wacher, Seth set out through the snow for the lodge of Black Horse.

The village was composed of at least a hundred lodges and possibly twice that many. It was impossible to tell without going among them, a feat he didn't feel compelled to perform. People were abroad, but mostly going from lodge to lodge. There was very little casual loitering. It was bitterly cold out. When Seth would look up and see the black eyes upon him, he would give stare for stare in the approved fashion. No one spoke to him until he was in Black Horse's lodge, then the big warrior gestured that he be seated. For a time neither man spoke, then Seth began, seeing the chieftain expected it. The difficulties of the language made talk brief and to the point.

"My brother and I have good hearts." Seth said laboriously. "We wish to hunt. We have no horses. We want to use Blackfoot horses to get meat."

Black Horse's obsidian glance, less glacial when they were alone, appeared to have a fleeting flicker of amusement in their oily depths. When he answered it was in astonishingly good English. Seth gaped and that brought the glint of laughter back to the Blackfoot's eyes again. "I lived two winters with white men. I know your tongue." He paused, evidently forming words he had to interpret from his own language before he spoke them.

"I will let you use my horses. You cannot go alone. Warriors of the Bloods will go hunting too—with you." Another pause. Black Horse's glance was thoughtful and appraising. "Why did you come to us?"

"We told you," Seth said in English. "Because of the storm."

Black Horse seemed to reflect over this but his glance never wavered in its intent regard of the white trapper. "Did you know you might be killed? We are not at war with your Grandfather [President of the United States; meaning, loosely, the Americans] but we fight your people. They are in our land. They take away our game. They have no right here."

Seth made a gesture that indicated he'd heard all that before many times. "This is a big country. There's enough room for all of us. Among my people there are many fools. Many who kill for the love of killing. It is not so with me. It isn't so with Beaver Killer. We are more Indian than white. We will prove it to you this winter."

Black Horse relaxed a little and bent his head, looking into the fire. "You have strong medicine," he said. "I do not hate white men. Only some. Only the blue-suits (soldiers) and those who harm us. We are strong people. Why don't the white men go somewhere else to trap and kill? This is a big land. Down south there is good hunting. This is our country."

Seth began working the dry-stiffness out of his lower pants legs as he talked. "I am only one white man. I am only a small white man. I am not a blue-suit. I am a trapper. What the Grandfather does I can't help. We are among you this winter without weapons, almost. All we want is a chance to stay alive through the cold time. For that we will always be your friends. If you don't trust us, at least give us a chance to prove to you that our hearts are good."

Black Horse looked up again. His glance was shrewd

46

and steady. "Did you know we had another white medicine-man with us?"

Seth shook his head without speaking. It seemed to make the prevarication less personal that way. Black Horse's glance didn't waver.

"He was taken by a war party. He had a female with him. She is his daughter."

"How do you know he is a medicine-man?"

"I didn't," Black Horse said. "I wasn't on that raid. It was the younger men, under Plume." The Blackfoot's glance went back to the fire-hole again. Seth thought he read something grim and unbending in the look before it swung away from him.

"The warriors would have killed all those people. As it was, some of them ran away and hid and the warriors never found them. They knew this white man was a medicine-man because he was taking care of a sick man all day while they watched the camp from a hiding place. They took him alive because white man medicine is strong and we have sickness too."

With as casual a tone as he could muster, Seth asked his next question. "Why did the Bloods take the female too?"

Black Horse scratched his thick, coarse hair when he answered. It was plaited into two braids that hung on either side of his head, down over his shoulders. "Plume did that. He is a great warrior. He brought her back for his slave." Black Horse stopped speaking after that and Seth could piece in the rest of it with reasonable clarity, for he knew the Siksika tolerably well.

Among the Blackfeet, chieftainship wasn't hereditary as it was among some races. In fact, a chieftain could be deposed at any time by another warrior outstanding enough to eclipse the war-honours and coups of the reigning leader. Obviously, Seth deduced, there was a behind-the-scenes battle going on between Black Horse and Plume.

He and Jules both had seen the animosity that existed between the two fighting men the night before, at the council. Now the reason for it was evident. Seth studied the chieftain's profile. It was the typical, strong face of a Blackfoot Indian. The nose was prominent and slightly hooked, the eyes were deep-set and jet black and the features were even, not unlike those of any white man. Taken as a whole, Black Horse was an intelligent, handsome Indian. His forehead jutted out over his eyes a little, and his square jaw was rounded where his chin jutted firm and solid.

"Plume brought back the girl to remind your people he's a great warrior. He brought back the white medicine-man to put his name upon their lips." This was said in the Algonquin tongue of the Blackfeet. Black Horse heard it, of course, but he held his silence. Didn't, in fact lift his head nor turn his glance away from the fire-hole. Seth let the silence grow between them, waiting.

Black Horse was a long time in speaking. When he did he had evidently thought of many things and come back again to the question of Seth and Jules being among his people. Reverting to his own language, but speaking it slowly, he told Seth it would be impossible to hunt until the snow at least melted partially. Seth agreed.

"But we must hunt. We will go afoot, but we must go a long way now."

Black Horse considered this for a moment, then grunted disapproval. "It is too cold. Wait. When Our Father (the sun) warms the marrow I will go with you."

"Our pemmican won't last that long."

Black Horse motioned towards some shiny, swollen buffalo paunches. "Take what you need from there. You can re-pay me later."

Seth looked at the chieftain soberly. "You don't want us to leave the camp for a while. All right. We don't know your reason. We trust our brother. All right. We will visit among the people. We will look for the sick."

48

"Hou," Black Horse said, getting to his feet. "Hou. Wait. I will go get the white medicine-man."

Seth re-crossed his legs with his heart pounding. He nodded with a perfectly blank look and waited until Black Horse had left the tipi, then he let the imprisoned air within him come out in a long, hissing sigh.

The wait was longer than Seth had expected, but when Black Horse came back there was a white man with him. Seth looked up, caught the quick, stabbing glance of the captive and noticed that his face was bruised and swollen; it was easy to guess the reason. Warriors weren't gentle people.

Maintaining the silence and avoiding the frankly curious stare of the medical man, Seth waited for Black Horse to seat himself again. The chief then looked from one to the other of them, and spoke in his halting English, which was good enough for the long pauses he was addicted to in between sentences.

"This is Medicine Walker. This is Bear."

Seth looked up then, and nodded very gravely. The captive was a man in his early forties, inclined to be fleshy around the middle. Seth thought grimly that he would lose that fat before the winter was out. No one over-ate in an Indian village. The doctor's eyes were wide and intensely blue with an absorbed way of looking at people as though he were measuring them. His hair was thinning but black. Shades lighter than Jules's hair, but still black.

"Mr. Bear?"

The doctor shook his head. "Baird. Doctor Baird." He seemed at a loss as to how to conduct himself and lapsed into silence again, studying Seth owlishly, without blinking.

"My name's Seth Wolff. My pardner and I are wintering with the Bloods. We heard about you last night when we came in." Seth was conscious of Black Horse's stare of concentration as the chieftain tried hard to follow the rapid flow of English.

Baird blinked. "You are prisoners, too?"

"No, we're just wintering with the Indians." Seth saw the instant veil of distrust and suspicion filter down over the doctor's glance. It made him flush. "We're trappers, Mister Baird, not renegades or squaw-men."

"But friendlies," Baird said softly, dryly.

Seth shrugged and longed to say more but couldn't. Not with Black Horse listening and watching. "Were you travelling through?"

"Yes. My daughter and I were on our way to Fort Bridger from Fort Union. We'd joined some other immigrants and were ambushed by Indians near the Musselshell river. The others were killed, I believe."

Seth shook his head. "Not all of them. Some got away." He flagged his head sideways. "Black Horse here, told me that much." Seth slid the next question in casually enough. "Your daughter—is she all right?"

Baird's eyes had a hopelessness in them Seth had seen in trapped animals; never before in a man. "She's a prisoner of an Indian named Plume. A slave, Mister Wolff."

"I know. You can't expect much else. But is she all right? I mean—well—healthy and unhurt—and all?"

Baird regarded Seth's face for a moment in silence, then he shrugged. "I'm not allowed to see her. Once in a while I catch sight of her, though. This Plume sends her to the creek to cut willows for his horses and forage for firewood. She appears to be holding up well, Mister Wolff."

"Call me Seth." The older man nodded with no particular interest. Seth sat back thoughtfully and looked at Black Horse. "Can I go with my brother to see his sick?"

The Blackfoot nodded without hesitation and Seth got up. Baird was watching them both for a cue as to what he should do next. Evidently he had learned to watch for such movements and obey quickly. The welts across his face indicated how Blackfoot discipline had been impressed upon him. Seth looked over at him and jerked his head toward the door-flap.

"Come on. Let's go. We'll visit the sick Injuns together."

They left the lodge and were instantly assaulted by the awful cold. Baird shivered in spite of himself and turned to look at Seth. He dutifully obeyed the motion Seth made and tramped in the soggy tracks of the trapper until they were among the little pathways among the tipis; then Seth stopped and turned toward him.

"Baird, I'm no doctor. My pardner told them that last night in council because they respect medicine-men of any kind. They're strong believers in medicine-men and preachers of any kind. You're damned lucky. They lay in ambush all day studying your immigrant encampment. If they hadn't done that and seen you takin' care of some sick immigrants, you'd be dead now." Seth fished out the little painting from his belt-pouch and palmed it so that the older man could see it. "Is that your daughter?"

Startled, Baird nodded briskly. "Yes. That's Karin." The intense blue eyes lifted quickly and stared at Seth's face. "Where did you get that?"

Seth didn't answer right away, and when he did there was a taint of anger in his voice. "Baird, I'm no renegade. If you think me'n my pardner were with those bucks you're wrong. I've told you the truth—up to a point. The rest of it's simply that after I came across the place where your party was ambushed, and found this painting, I decided to see if you were still alive—not you exactly, but her. That's why my pardner an' me came into this village."

Baird listened with the faint flame of hope lighting his glance. He made a nervous little motion with one arm. "Do you think there's a chance of getting out of here?"

"No," Seth said brutally, still resentful. "Not until spring. We couldn't get ten miles in this snow. They'd run us down an' kill every one of us."

"Till spring," the doctor said vaguely, looking past

Seth's shoulders at the Blackfoot village. There was despair and fear in his glance and Seth saw it. That annoyed him even more.

"What the hell're you worrying about? How about your daughter? She'll have a lot to regret before then; not you. All you have to do is take care of colds and bellyaches."

Seth turned away angrily and trudged on through the snow until at least part of his anger had subsided, then he stopped, waited for the older man to catch up, and nodded toward the tipis. "Which one's got a sick Injun in it? We got to make this look like two medicine men're making their rounds. Afterwards, if no one stops us, we'll go back down to my lodge and talk."

Baird led Seth in silence after that. His dark blue eyes weren't apathetic, but they showed no hope either. They visited several lodges where sick Bloods were. One was patently a case of chronic drunkenness.

After the wet, weak circle of the sun came through this dismal overcast and worried away with sickly heat at the fringes of the snow pack, they retraced their steps and went back down to the lodge where Jules sat, feeding the little fire and nursing his cold shanks. He looked up at the stranger's entrance and waited until Seth had explained everything, then he motioned the doctor down and studied him openly and frankly. He shook his head at Seth.

"Thus 'un couldn't run a mile, boy. You've saddled us with two stones."

Seth grunted and hunkered. "Can't get out till spring anyway, Jules."

Placidly, Jules went back to toasting his legs. "Then we got to hunt, for my pemmican's 'bout gone."

Baird hadn't spoken. When he did it was with the same despair that had annoyed Seth. "Mister—ah—Jules?"

The trapper smiled at him. "Just plain Jules. The rest of it don't matter. Almost forgot it m'self."

"Well—"

"If you're goin' to ask about our chances," Jules said, then stopped right there and made an apologetic little shrug with his shoulders and showed both hands, palms upwards. He raised his glance to Seth, saw the lingering anger there and looked back at Baird again. "Make the best of it, Baird. They won't starve you. About the girl," his dark eyes flickered to Seth and he hesitated before going on. "They'll work the devil out of her. They always do to prisoners. But if she's stout enough she'll make it."

They fed Baird from the shrinking supply of pemmican and watched him wander out again after finding out which lodge he was in. Then Jules sat patiently waiting for the younger man to speak. Seth did, around the stem of his stone pipe.

"Black Horse and Plume, as I got it figured, are having a sort of tug-of-war over the leadership of the band, Jules."

"It'd be somethin' like that," Jules said. "An' the girl's Plume's prisoner. How's Black Horse?"

"Seems friendly enough. Suspicious as hell though."

"You can't blame him, boy. They've got no call to love whites. No Siksika has."

"He speaks damned good English. Told me he'd lived two winters among the whites. Nearly surprised me to death."

Jules grunted, eyes round. "Thunderation," he said in amazement. " 'Tain't common at all."

Seth looked up and smiled slightly at Jules's amazement. The smile didn't stay long. "Jules, I've been thinking. Plume owns the girl. The man's safe enough—anyway, he rubs my fur the wrong way a little."

"You can't blame him. He's scairt stiff and ever'thing's strange to him. He's a immigrant, Seth. They're like bighorn sheep. Fearful all the time."

"The girl's in a bad spot. If Black Horse wasn't near fighting with Plume it'd be different."

53

Jules screwed up his face in concentration. "Seth, you daren't try to help her too much. I'm warning you, boy. Blackfeet're coyotes. They're smarter than you think. Smart as a white man, some of 'em."

Seth looked up with annoyance. "I know that," he said. They both lapsed into silence. It lasted until Seth got up and moved restlessly around the lodge under Jules's contemplative stare, then went back out into the snow. The sun had come out with a vengeance. It made him wince away from the merciless reflection off the snow. Indians were moving among the tipis and the long, eerie silence was broken by the customary commotion of a Blackfoot village.

Dogs ran through the snow-aisles and the bedlam of squaws at work, drying robes, cleaning out lodges, the while they screamed at weasel-eyed youngsters who were running amuck in their new-found freedom, added to the colourful scene. Seth stood back and ignored the openly curious stares he got. Men headed past in the direction of the horse herd carrying twisted grass and horsehair bridles, Some even carried the light, almost shapeless, buffalo-hunter saddles.

From beyond the eastern fringes of the village came the shouts of men and boys. Seth guessed the creek would be over there and the men, addicted to daily baths summer and winter in the icy mountain streams, were over there bathing. With a sudden thought, he moved across the slushy lane before his lodge and headed towards the creek. The shouts were more numerous and closer, as he covered the distance.

The picture there was one of dignity abandoned and good natured raillery. Men derided one another's timidness in going into the ice-choked little creek. Others splashed water on the hesitant and laughed uproariously at the shock they caused. When Seth was close enough for them to recognise him as one of the white men among them, the noise gradually died away. The Bloods watched him without appearing to.

Very methodically he strolled along the creek bank until he was past where most of the men were bathing. There were boys and youngsters farther up the creek. He stopped and watched them. The ordeal of bathing, here, was a duty, not a source of amusement nor invigoration. The little dark faces with their glistening black eyes were full of grim determination and nothing else. Seth smiled. The boys eyed him askance and locked their jaws so the white man wouldn't see their teeth chattering behind blue lips.

He sat upon a dead-fall and watched them. Very gradually he looked up the creek where the women were. They too, were bathing, but the sounds were vastly different. More like the scream of a bitch-raccoon caught in a trap. High and shrill and with a shrieking timbre that rasped crossways over Seth's eardrums and made him shudder at the sound.

The bodies up there were dark. He looked a long time but saw nothing that would be a white woman. Swinging back towards the boys, he was conscious of men coming behind him. Twisting a little, he watched Plume and several other warriors come down near him. He saw them stop when they noticed him, stare granite-eyed, then move on as though he didn't exist, go to the willow stumps and strip. Appraising the powerful body of Plume, Seth reluctantly admired the rippling, tawny power of the Blood warrior.

The men hesitated a little at the water's edge, but Plume, conscious of Medicine-Walker's glance, walked slowly and unfalteringly out into the deepest part, turned majestically and gave Seth stare for stare as he slowly sat down among the ice particles. Seth had to grunt to himself in admiration, for the Blood's expression hadn't altered one iota. His control was typical of Plains Indians, but immeasurably better than most.

The men bathed without horseplay. Seth understood his presence caused this ridiculousness of great dignity while turning blue, and smiled a little at it. The women were shrieking again, indicating more had come down to the creek to bathe, but he ignored it, watching Plume instead. The big warrior washed himself very methodically, then turned his head to listen to something said softly by one of his companions. The other Indians smiled. Seth knew they had all heard it.

Plume straightened up and looked across at Seth. In Siksika he spoke very clearly, so that even the women could hear him. "Does my white brother fear the cold water or is he too clean to need it?"

Seth studied the man calmly. Plume had shown his own vast control and was now, at the instigation of his interested friends, inviting the white man to show his strongheart. Seth sat there until the Indians began to smile derisively at him, then he got up and tugged off his hunting shirt, folded it very carefully and laid it on the rock. The men and boys let a ripple of approval and anticipation run among them. Without glancing once at his challenger, he stripped to the hide and turned slowly, dragging out every second of the scene in true Indian fashion. He wrung all the drama from it he could.

Standing naked and erect, he crossed glances with the Blood warrior. They were of a size. Their bodies, different in hue, were equally packed with hard, fluid muscle that rippled with each movement. The boys made their eyes round at the obvious strength of the white man. The warriors were less inclined to show what they noticed, but they looked just the same.

Then, very slowly. . . . Even more slowly than Plume had done, Seth advanced to the water's edge and kept right on going. The chill was at once so shocking and congealing that it made his breath come in tiny convulsions. He moved very slowly, summoning all the decorum he could, facing Plume without moving a facial muscle or batting an eye until he was directly in front of the buck.

Then he squatted, eased down into the water with teeth locked and jaw muscles bunched in a hard paralysis, and completely submerged himself.

He stood up once more and faced the Blackfoot. Plume hadn't wet his head or face. Seth had.

The warriors voiced their admiration with guttural grunts. One said something in English that he quite obviously had no knowledge of the meaning of, but used to indicate approval. He had more than likely been taught by some fun-loving trappers sometime, because it was enough to make the average white man turn and stare.

Plume's impassive features didn't alter. Even after he turned away from Seth and went over near his friends where he would complete his bath. Seth's defiant blankness didn't alter either. Not until he turned back towards the bank—and saw the intensely blue eyes of the white girl, regarding him with amazement.

He dropped into the water like a stone and sat there with only his upper body visible. What a hell of an introduction!

They stared at one another for a long minute. Seth knew her instantly. He knew something else just as quickly too. Jules had been wrong. This girl had the identical beauty the picture had depicted. Only one thing was different. Her eyes were deeper blue, as the doctor's eyes were, only more so. Almost violet in colour. Her face had the strong roundness and the youthful, breath-taking handsomeness the painter of the little miniature had captured so well.

Seth stirred a little and felt the awful cold. He spoke with an effort to control the instinctive chattering of his teeth. "Is your name Baird?"

She nodded at him. Evidently she, too, had come down to bathe. Her clothing was all but in shreds. One leg was bare from the ankle to slightly above the knee and a painful looking scratch ran the full distance of her flesh where some spine had ripped at her.

"I'm Karin Baird. Who are you?"

"Seth Wolff. My pardner and I came in here last night."

Her stare held to his face. If she had been going to say more she didn't get the chance. A squaw Seth recognised as Plume's Sits-Beside-Him-Woman came up and nudged Karin Baird, then gestured toward the water and spoke to her in Siksika. The girl lowered her head and shot Seth a questioning look from under her lashes. "What did she say?"

"That you've got to bathe like the rest of them do." He splashed water over his chest and rubbed vigorously, and spoke as he did it. "Injuns don't mind this sort of thing, but I guess you mind it a little. Turn your back so's I can get out, Karin, and I'll leave." He spoke matter-of-factly; this was no time for foolish embarrassment.

Without answering the girl faced away from him. Seth stood up and made his way to the bank, shook himself Indian fashion, like a wet dog, and brushing off the surplus water with the edge of his hands, dressed himself. He didn't glance at Plume or the other Bloods as he trudged back toward the village through the snow.

He passed Indians without bothering to even look up at them, and ignored the snapping, snarling, frenzied Blood dogs that went into paroxysms of excitement when the man in fringed buckskins, with the strange, unfamiliar smell, went by.

He stepped into his lodge and saw that Jules had taken a snow-bath. The fragrance of the old trapper's kinnikinnick filled the place. "I've seen her, Jules."

Jules removed the pipe slowly and looked closely at Seth's face, then put the pipe back into his mouth and went on smoking.

"You're wrong, too." He fished out the little picture and looked at it as he squatted by the fire-hole. "She looks exactly like the painting, Jules, only prettier." He raised his glance. "You said they didn't look like this, recall?"

Jules nodded, still without speaking. His glance was tolerant and perfectly calm.

"But she does, Jules."

Jules smoked on, still holding his silence and only occasionally looking over at Seth, but the younger man went right on speaking, until he caught the faintest sheen of amusement in his friend's eyes. Then he closed up and pouched the little painting again. He stayed silent for upwards of half an hour, then he broke the silence with a startling remark.

"Jules, we've got to get her out of here before spring."

The trapper took the pipe from his mouth very carefully and knocked out the dottle into the fire-hole. "You're ruttin', Seth," he said calmly. "If you could—if you could make it plumb away—where'd you take her?" His dark eyes were censorious. "You'd find no help 'twixt here and Gabe's Fort, if you could make it, which you couldn't. And what about her father? That old bull's got too much tallow around his middle t'run a mile, and you know it, boy." In a different tone of voice, Jules went on reproachfully. "You're not usin' your head, Seth—and I'm surprised at you."

Everything Jules said was painfully true. Seth knew it even as he listened. Their situation was hopeless until the spring thaws came. He swore with feeling and cast about for an alternative. There was none. He looked at the older man. "Wouldn't dare try to buy her from Plume?"

"No," Jules agreed, just as calmly. Then he stood up. "Snow's melted enough. Let's go hunting."

Seth understood the purpose of Jules's suggestion but welcomed the activity nonetheless. They went to Black Horse's lodge with their long-rifles and the chief joined them. His preparations were simple. He took down his arrow quiver and his un-strung bow—no fighting Indian

59

ever left his hunting- or war-bow strung during damp weather—and went out into the snow with them.

Seth had figured the chief would call a few Blood hunters to accompany them. Black Horse evidently disdained to do this, however, and the three of them struck out across the slippery valley-land heading due west, where the horse herders, mostly boys in their early teens, were holding the large Blackfoot remuda and constantly moving it in the desperate search for winter feed.

Catching and mounting Black Horse's animals didn't take long. The chieftain held his arm aloft, northward. "Meat—there. Long ride but good hunting."

Jules rode beside Seth with Black Horse on the farthest side of him. They saw much sign of other hunting parties out ahead of them, but they had to ride until the other horse imprints were few before they could expect to find much.

Near the Belts, they struck westward and Black Horse finally strung his short bow made of fused buffalo horns. After that they rode in single file until they were atop a series of ridges that went crookedly along, due north, following the upthrusts of the serrated little arroyos below them. Rarely speaking, the three men never drew rein until the warrior pulled up and pointed off to their left, down across the immediate gullies and far out over the plain.

"Buffalo."

Seth saw only tiny shapes in the immense distance, but he assumed their identification on the same basis Black Horse and Jules did. They were meandering along the trail that Jules and Seth had travelled shortly before. Heading, possibly, toward the salt-lick farther down-country.

Jules speculated on the distance. "It's a long way off," he said.

Seth grunted at him. "What's the difference? Let's go." He reined around the Blackfoot and struck down across the little humps of land, riding slantingly downward to

60

make a fall in the slippery footing less likely, then, down in the widening valley that led upwards to the vast Teton Basin, he lifted his mount into an easy lope and kept him at it.

They rode two full hours, making good time, before Black Horse held his arm up and stopped his horse. "I smell them," he said. "Not far now. Leave the horses here."

They dismounted, tied their animals in the willows along a dry-wash full of muddy snow-water, and went along behind Seth in a jog-trot towards the nearest little hillock.

CHAPTER FOUR

SETH worked his way up the hill with considerable effort. The earth was sticky and spongy, making solid footing impossible. He was perspiring in spite of the cold by the time he got to the ridge and squatted, waiting for Jules and Black Horse. The sight below him was enough to make any hunter's heart beat fast. The buffalo were down there by the hundreds. They weren't fat but they could still provide a good supply of meat. They couldn't scent the hunters overhead and in consequence were ambling along with twin jets of steam indicating where their nostrils were partially buried under the great mattress of dark hair.

Black Horse made an exclamation of pure elation. "Good. We should get much meat here. What we can't carry we'll send the squaws back for." He raised his bow, took long aim, and fired off the stubby arrow.

The might of the man behind the bow coupled to the tremendous pull of a good war-bow, sent the shaft deep into the side of a yearling cow. She emitted a startled snort, bawled and plunged into the herd. The other beasts stopped in quick fear and bewilderment. They milled a little, looking belligerently around.

Jules was prone, sighting, when the little cow came out of the herd with the broken shaft dangling, and went down very slowly, front legs first, then hind legs, as though lying down to chew her cud. She lowered her head until the snout was inches off the muddy earth, and there she died.

Seth was smiling, rolling two rifle balls around in his mouth for facilitating re-loading. He was watching Jules's unerring aim, just as Black Horse was, with great anticipation and interest, when something moving across the little canyon from them caught his attention. It wasn't a buffalo because it was higher than the straggling herd.

He watched for it again and, just as Jules's gun exploded, he saw the body of a man stand straight up, bowstring pulled back to chin. Startled and motionless, the Indian froze at the sound of the shot, then in a flash he was hidden among the brush across the way. Seth reached over and touched Jules without looking down.

"There's an Indian across the valley. Watch up there by the—" He said no more. All three of them saw the same thing at the same time. It wasn't one Indian hunter, it was a party of them. They weren't Blackfeet either. Jules erupted into livid profanity when the bucks opposite them stood up and raised the yell.

"Flatheads, boys. Goddam Flathead hunting party. Let's cache! " Without waiting to see what the others would do, Jules squirmed around and fled down the incline. Black Horse hesitated long enough to look at Seth.

"We go! "

Seth didn't answer. He sprinted after the Blood chieftain. Both of them caught up with Jules and raced beside him toward their horses. Seth kept a slanting watch up the hillside as he untied his animal with stiff-cold fingers. He was badly shaken but it didn't show in his voice. "They'll be a while. The buffalo're between them an' us."

Jules whipped his horse around and leapt into the saddle with a curse. "Buffalo won't bother 'em. Not when there's only three of us."

Seth mounted more leisurely, turned to watch Black Horse swing up, then cast a final glance up the hill. What he saw horrified him. By some incredible feat the Flatheads had breached the line of buffalo and were even then streaming down the hillside. Until Seth gave a yell to warn his companions of the imminence of danger, the Flatheads hadn't made a sound. Now they erupted into wild war cries, brandished their bows—and a rare few muskets—and kicked their animals out in a recklessly wild plunge down the slippery hillside.

"Run fer it," Jules yelled, and bent low over his horse's neck as he lit out back the way they had come. Black Horse and Seth were neck-and-neck, faces taut and defiant. Seth twisted backwards once and tried to estimate the numbers pursuing them. There were at least eight Flatheads, and probably more. Eight, nine, ten. . . . There was no time to make sure.

What contributed the most to the eventual defeat of the three hunters was the fact that Seth had led them in a stiff race toward the buffalo in the last stages of their hunt. Now their horses, still winded and not strong anyway, from their starvation-subsistence diet of willows, weakened fast.

The first Seth knew that the Flathead warriors were gaining on them was when an arrow struck a stone ahead of him and broke in two. He risked another glance back—and his heart sank. The hostiles were easily within bow range and well within musket range. He shot a glance ahead at old Jules. The trapper was quirting his horse with merciless, rhythmic strokes of his gun-butt.

Black Horse's animal pulled slightly ahead of Seth. The Siksika leader looked back at the Flatheads, then glanced briefly at Seth. His lips were drawn back in wolfish defiance, but even as Seth watched, he began to chant his war-song.

Seth cast about desperately for a place to make a stand. Up ahead of Jules was a little gully with some random boulders at the mouth of it. He waved his arm toward the place and yelled to Jules. "Cache, Jules!"

The trapper looked back at the Flatheads and made his decision instantly. The horse he was riding stumbled and recovered himself when the mountain man's heavy hand on the bridle-rein jerked him ruthlessly toward the little arroyo. Seth was kicking his legs wide of his mount when

Black Horse's animal gave a prodigious lurch in the air and collapsed under its rider. The Blackfoot was thrown through the air with arms and legs askew. Seth barely had time to swerve and avoid riding down the stunned chieftain, then he hooked one moccasined foot into the bony flank of his own mount, swept low and grabbed wildly at the Indian's hunting shirt.

Unable to lift the chieftain, Seth held his horse's mane with his rifle hand, with all the strength he had, and thundered toward the place where Jules had already abandoned his own mount and was standing wide-legged, spitting a ball down the barrel of his rifle.

Close enough, Seth let the Blackfoot drop and followed him to the ground in a sprawling leap, rolled quickly away from the churning hooves and fought his way to his knee. The Flatheads were yipping their short, explosive victory yelp when Seth brought his rifle to shoulder and fired. A buck with long braids of hair encased in otterskin threw up his arms and went over backwards off his horse.

The yelps stopped as abruptly as the Flatheads had materialised. The enemies wrenched their horses around to get out of rifle-range, but Seth was re-loading and Jules was kneeling, his rifle barrel resting steadily on a mossy boulder. Seth watched the smooth tracking of the barrel, then Jules fired. A Flathead let out a wild shout and went forward grasping blindly at his running horse's mane, missed it and fell forward off the left side of the animal, directly in the path of his companions. Jules straightened up and let off a defiant, triumphant Shoshoni war-cry.

Seth and Jules alternated. Having single-shot muskets and being wise in the ways of Indian warfare, neither man fired until the other was re-loading. In that way there was always one rifle ready to pick off a bold aggressor.

When the Flatheads had sent back their horses under guard of one of their fellow hunters, the rest came forward afoot. Jules watched them and made a wry face, spat and jerked his head around towards Seth.

"They's more than enough of 'em, Seth. Mind they don't get above us." He shot a look at Black Horse and curled his mouth downward caustically. "Hell of a time for him to leave us."

Seth went over and dug into a crevasse where some snow had escaped the sun's rays. He patted the snow into the shape of a pancake and held it against the side of Black Horse's head. It took a long time to bring the warrior back to consciousness, but when the black eyes finally opened, Seth threw away the snow and held out the Blackfoot's heavy little war bow. "Come on; we got a fight on our hands." Then he turned away from the Indian and ignored him.

Black Horse held his head in his hands for a few minutes before he twisted around and looked at Seth and Jules, both of whom avoided him completely, thus allowing the chieftain a moment to collect his wits without embarrassment. Then he moved slowly toward them, glancing beyond their bulwark of rock and earth where the Flatheads were shouting taunts and shooting arrows against their position.

Jules kept up a continuous fire, alternating with Seth's gunfire, until Black Horse was huddled beside a large boulder, then the old trapper loaded his gun and held it in his hands, looking over at Seth.

"They'll slip up an' slit our gullets come sundown, Seth. We daren't stay here too long."

Seth glanced briefly at Jules, then back at the hiding places of the Flatheads. "What do you reckon we can do, Jules? Even if we catch the damned horses, they aren't strong enough to pack us back to the Blood village—you saw that before."

Jules looked cautiously around his boulder then grunted. "I don't know, boy," he said, "but we're sunk ducks if we keep this up."

Seth squirmed down next to the Blackfoot. "Black Horse. How can we get away from here?"

66

The warrior looked around them and back to Seth's face. "There is no way. They'll be around us if they aren't already. There is no way."

Seth placed his rifle between two crumbling rocks and waited for a target. He was seething inside. Being killed in such an obscure little gully by such known cowards as the Flathead Indians made him hot with anger. He lay there waiting for a target that never presented itself. The attackers had learnt caution. Three of their party were sprawled in the mud, dead.

The lull in the firing became total. Even the Flathead hunters weren't loosing their arrows and those with muskets, aside from the noise they made, were absolutely harmless. They either flinched away when they pulled their triggers, or had no sights on their guns, for not once did a ball strike the rocks or mud close to the embattled white men and the lone Blackfoot.

Jules was swearing in his colourful mixture of many tongues when Seth canted his head for a cocked glance up at the grey sky. The disc of the sun not only wasn't giving out heat any longer, but it was also sliding far off toward the western mountains, inexorably. He looked at his two companions. Jules was tiring. Seth could tell it from the weary way he moved his head in the search for foemen. Black Horse was grim of visage and woefully low on arrows. Seth had every indication of the inevitable end around him. He swung abruptly away from his gun-port among the boulders and reached far over to brush Jules's arm. The old trapper swung a face shiny with coagulated sweat. His dark eyes were questioning, in a dull way.

"I'm going to try something. Keep them busy." With that, Seth began to squirm through the old grass and icy mud away from them. He turned once and looked over his shoulder. Both Jules and Black Horse were staring after him. He made an angry pantomime for them to keep on shooting; reluctantly, begrudgingly, the Indian turned back and searched for the Flatheads. He said something to Jules and Seth could see the old trapper's expression undergo a radical change. What Jules said back wasn't discernible, but the indignation on his face was explanation enough.

Seth swung back and continued to worm his way up the little gully. He became literally plastered with frozen mud. The cold stole into his muscles gradually, so that in time it slowed his progress; it made him conscious of its dragging weight, but by then he was far east and swinging in a large circle northward above the Flatheads.

The sound of the battle was clear and distinct because the air was so brittle, but Seth knew it was a long way behind him when he dragged his aching length in behind some chapparral and gazed down over the slope. With no difficulty at all he could count eight Flatheads. There had been eleven of them in the hunting party.

He itched to shoot one in the back and drive the rest out into the open, but that was doubtful strategy.

Off another quarter mile, squatting and wrapped in his blanket was the horse guard. Seth concentrated on him and saw the graceful tilt of a long-rifle cradled in the Indian's arms. He grimaced. It was going to be easier than he had anticipated. An uneasy glance at the sinking sun, though, drove him on.

Unfortunately, the horse guard was alert. He was a 'breed of some kind and wore his hair in the roach so rarely seen in the far northwest. Seth lay half in, half out, of a little snow freshet with the icewater and clay-mud running over his lower legs, watching the Flathead. The Indian would stand up once in a while and peer down toward the sound of the fight. When a war cry would ripple back to him, he became especially agitated and would walk a little way toward the sound of conflict then come trudging back with a restless, fierce glance at the horses. The animals were tied among the willows by their single rein, grazing as best they could.

Seth knew there was no way to get close enough to

close with the buck. Neither did he dare risk the noise of a shot. He lay watching the buck until he squatted again, facing towards the sound of the fight, southward. Then Seth arose very carefully, drew out his hatchet, hefted it, flexed his shoulder muscles, lifted it and brought his arm overhand in a smooth, graceful arc.

The weapon spun end over end in the dying daylight. The Flathead jumped high into the air when the thing struck him, and half turned. Seth was vaulting toward him with giant strides. The Flathead fought against the numbing effects of the blow and sank to his knees, stubbornly fighting against the nausea that was going over him in waves.

Seth scooped up the hatchet as the Indian brought his gun up. A violent, sideways chopping sweep knocked the gunbarrel aside. A second vicious sweep with the tomahawk and the Flathead collapsed.

Seth sucked in great gulps of icy air and hesitated only long enough to snatch away the Flathead's rifle and powder-horn with the bullet-pouch attached to it by a damp thong. Then he turned to the horses. Slashed at their reins and swung atop the sturdiest looking one of the lot, edged in behind them and raised the yell.

Instantly the horses struck out in a panicked run and Seth stayed close up, lashing out freely, stirring them to greater efforts. He threw his head back and let out a wild Blackfoot cry that echoed and re-echoed down through the canyon and rose above the pounding drumroll of the horses' hooves.

Somewhere up ahead an answering shout broke into the confusion but it was a wail, ending with a long, dismal "ey-eeee!"

Racing low over his horse in the wake of the Flathead buffalo-horses, Seth caught a flash of a wildly running Flathead. The man's face was a mask of terror as he saw the horses being herded straight at him. He had his bow in one hand but made no attempt to use it. Seth raised his rifle, took long aim and fired. The Flathead stumbled but kept on running until he was half-way up the hillside, then he slowed to a staggering trot and finally fell in a heap.

The Flatheads were crying out loudly and running to get clear of their herded horses. Twice, Seth heard the unmistakable roar of Jules's rifle. He re-loaded his own piece and held it in his right hand. The undulating victory cry of the Siksika broke over the nearer noise. Black Horse was out in the open, running toward Seth waving his blanket. The Flathead horses went stiff-legged in their attempt to halt but their forward momentum, added to the greasy mud underfoot, let them slide almost up to Black Horse. The big Blackfoot caught one animal by the mane and swung aboard him. It was all done in single, fluid, graceful movement.

Seth circled the horses at a slow lope. Held them milling until Jules came up, the weariness gone from his face and the sweat-sheen of it shiny in the bloody sunset so that he looked as much an Indian as Black Horse did.

They kept the Flathead horses moving after they were mounted. Drove them in a wild run straight toward the bivouac of the Bloods at Moon Prairie. Nor did they stop until the sounds of their wild cries brought the men and women tumbling from their lodges. Seth reined off a little way from Jules and Black Horse and galloped his Flathead horse in a small, tight little circle. This was the traditional signal used among the Plains Indians to indicate that the rider had sighted an enemy and knew where he was. It was, in effect, the call to arms.

With elated shouts the Bloods ran for their weapons while their squaws trotted for the war horses. It didn't take long for the mounted war party to race up beside Seth. He looked past them and saw Jules wave a tired arm at him, motioning him on. Black Horse, eyes shining with the excitement, covered with mud and with a thick clot of blood in the tumble of his hair where his fall had brought him up against a rock, shouted in English. "Let's go. Plenty coup back there."

Seth turned and belaboured the captured horse. The Bloods streamed behind him in full-throated cry. They rode hard, for the sun was fast fading over the horizon. Seth knew the Flatheads wouldn't be there when they returned and he wasn't wrong.

While the others scalped the fallen men Seth rode over and, with a smile, handed Black Horse the Flathead gun, pouch, and powder horn. Then he spun his horse and went looking for sign. It wasn't hard to find in the trodden, spongy earth. With a shout, Seth motioned the Bloods to follow. He raced up the hill over which the Flatheads had come in full cry only a few hours before. Down below, where two buffalo carcasses lay, were the unhorsed hostiles. They were as ready as they could get for what they had known was coming, as soon as they had heard the first Blackfoot war-cry.

Seth sat his horse and waited. The Bloods charged down the hill in a jumble of eager fighting men. The Flatheads loosed arrows but the avengers never wavered. Seth saw the warrior, Plume, far in the lead. He watched when the fearless Blackfoot charged his horse right into the Flathead's little fort and bent far to one side to strike out with his bow. To strike an enemy in battle with the hand or with something held in the hand, was the supreme insult a warrior could offer another fighting man. It was also the greatest of war honours. Seth watched Plume's zig-zagging course as he raced back towards his companions, who were firing and shouting exultingly as they closed with the Flatheads.

Seth saw Black Horse break away from the band to duplicate Plume's trick. He didn't make it though. His horse collapsed for the second time that day, shot out from under him. He staggered to his feet and fired his rifle into the enemy, then was lost in the swirl of riders as his Blood warriors raced by, screaming at the top of their voices.

Seth eased his winded Flathead horse down the slope slowly. He had no desire to be in at the finish. Nor was he. By the time he got to where the methodical Bloods were cutting the throats of the dead buffalo, as an afterthought to the other blood-letting, it was all over. Limp, bloody scalps were tied to bows and rifles, and even to the chin parts of the Blackfoot war-bridles. Black Horse, his face split wide in a victorious grin, kneed his dripping Flathead horse over beside Seth.

"Much honour here." He said it in his native tongue. Seth nodded, looking at the dead Flatheads. They had been stripped bare and scalped. He made a motion toward the buffalo and glanced up at Black Horse's face.

"Let's take this back with us."

Black Horse blinked at Seth, his big smile withering. He didn't take his glance off the white man until Seth had dismounted and gone to work on the closest buffalo. Fleshing under the great shaggy hide, he worked with the long sweeping strokes of a knife wielder used to skinning large animals. Then Black Horse turned and called to his warriors. All but Plume came over. The chieftain pointed with his chin towards Seth, but said nothing. The bucks understood, made their weapons and trophies secure to their belts and went to work.

Seth straightened up when a Blackfoot took over. He looked at Black Horse, and saw Plume sitting his horse beyond the chieftain. Their glances met, held, and Seth turned away with a solid shaft of hatred, like flame, mirrored in his glance. He went to his horse, swung up and rode over beside the leader. Black Horse was tentatively exploring the side of his head with muddy fingers.

"Plenty coup," the chief said.

"Yeh," Seth said. "Ride back with me. The warriors will bring the meat."

Black Horse looked at Seth with a sobering regard, then he nodded quite abruptly, swung his horse and started along at a slow walk beside the white man. Seth said nothing until they were well beyond the farthest Indian, then he twisted and looked back. Everyone was working but Plume. The great warrior was sitting just as motionless and erect as ever.

"Sits like a chief, doesn't he?"

Seth watched Black Horse's reaction. Saw the quick rush of angry blood under the dusky hide and swung his glance away when Black Horse peered over at him. There was death in the black eyes of the Blood leader. "Chief? Plume long time want to be chief."

Seth rode along in silence until they were close to the village, then he looked around at Black Horse and saw that most of the black storminess had vanished. "Ten Flathead horses," he said, by way of an opener. By Blackfoot standards they should all belong to the man who had taken them. This was even more true in Seth's case, for except for his arduous and risky trek around the Flathead warriors, all three of them might very well be dead.

Black Horse studied the white man without speaking. The Flathead horses, to a Siksika, most renowned of horsethieves, were a mighty coup in themselves. Mightier even than Plume's valorous act of striking a Flathead foeman with his bow.

Seth turned and met the big warrior's gaze. "I got the horses. I got behind the Flatheads and routed them. Chased them out into the open. The horses are my coup."

He watched Black Horse's face. Saw the tightening around the mouth that hid the droop and the slight puckering, up around the obsidian eyes.

"Black Horse, my heart is good," Seth said in Siksika. "My heart is strong. I am your brother. I saved your life today. I give you my coup."

But Black Horse's gratitude didn't extend beyond acceptance. He nodded his head gravely to indicate solemn appreciation. "Medicine-Walker," he said very formally, "is my brother. He is a great warrior. What the Bloods have is his."

Then Seth struck. "Black Horse, I wish to buy the captive girl from Plume. He is not your friend. He is not my friend. I no longer have Flathead horses to buy the girl with because I have given them to my brother."

Black Horse was startled and showed it. "Why do you want this woman? She is a slave. Among the Bloods are better women. Medicine-Walker can claim a Sits-Beside-Him-Woman from among them."

"No," Seth said stubbornly. "I want this white woman. We are of the same blood."

"I can't help you," Black Horse said quickly, in English. "She belongs to Plume."

"I know. Tell me how I can get her from him?"

Black Horse rode all of a mile lost in thought. He had a great debt to repay and was very conscious of it. At last he raised his head and looked at the village coming toward them as they rode through the last rays of early twilight. The smell of wood smoke was strong in the air.

"There is no way. He will not sell her. He never sells captives. They are his coups. He is a proud warrior."

Seth made a dour face in the shadows. Plume wanted his captives before the people of his band to remind them always of his prowess. Something about the man's tremendous vanity struck Seth forcibly, like a tangible blow with an open hand. Stung him to greater than ever dislike of the warrior.

"No horses? No guns? Nothing?"

"Nothing. Plume is a proud man." Black Horse said it so simply and with such finality that Seth looked around at him. The warrior's profile was stony, facing ahead toward the village. Seth studied the Blood's face and looked away from it with a surge of fierce anger making him almost shake. The chieftain was his friend. He was grateful. He was convinced of Seth's courage and worth.

Up to a point. He would *not* be a party to anything that was against *morēs* of his people.

They rode the rest of the way back to the village in absolute silence. Only when they turned their horses loose in the band of Blood animals and turned to trudge back into the village, where the bedlam of a great celebration was getting under way, did either man look at the other. Then Black Horse faced Seth outside the lodge the two white trappers shared. His look was level and unwavering.

"You are a strong-heart," he said in Siksika. "You have proven yourself. So has Beaver Killer. You have nothing to fear from the Bloods. But Plume will kill the white woman if he knows you want her. I will say nothing. You will say nothing. That way she will live. I have spoken."

Seth nodded but said nothing at all, turned abruptly on his heel and entered the lodge. Immediately he was struck by an aroma of roasting meat and the full impact of his hunger hit him so suddenly he felt a little lightheaded. Jules glanced up with a smile. His stone pipe was making an altogether different aroma too.

"Some squaws brang us this hunk o' butt meat." He said it so simply that Seth got the impression the old trapper had already forgotten about their nearly fatal skirmish with the hostile Flatheads.

Jules sliced the meat and handed Seth a long, savoury strip of it. "You fetch in the buffaloes we killed?"

"The Blood warriors're bringing them back."

"Did they massacre them Flathead devils?"

Seth nodded. "Every last one of 'em, Jules. Lord, I'm hungry."

Jules cut more meat and held it out to the younger man on the tip of his skinning knife. "We're safe now, boy. Them bucks grinned at me so wide I could see their innards. Nothing to worry about now, but the spring thaws an' leavin' in time to make it to Pierre's Hole for the rendezvous."

"And," Seth said softly, "Karin Baird."

Jules made a quick gesture of annoyance. "I forgot her. Her an' her daddy." He hunkered over the roast, watching it cook above the fire-hole on a green willow spit, with professional care. "I don't reckon it'll be hard to get her now. We got Flathead horses to buy her with."

Seth told how he had gambled on Black Horse—and lost. Jules listened wide-eyed. "You mean he took the critters then wouldn't help you get her?"

"Yeh. Wouldn't or couldn't—I don't know which. If Plume wasn't priming himself for Black Horse's chieftainship, I think he'd have helped us, but Plume's too big a warrior." He told Jules about the Blackfoot's coup against the embattled Flatheads. The old trapper snorted in scorn.

"Godalmighty, Seth; I seen 'em do that hundreds of times. It ain't brave—it's tomfoolish." He lapsed into a gloomy silence and poked irritably at the roast. "Now we're afoot again."

"I'm sorry, Jules."

The trapper's black eyes lifted hurriedly. He managed a grin, but it wasn't too successful and he let it evaporate. " 'Tain't nothing, Seth. Anyway, we're big bucks among 'em now." Then Jules swore scathingly and said something that indicated his true feelings right then. "An' after you hauled his black carcass out from in front of them root-eatin' Flatheads, too. Damn his Black Horse heart, anyway."

They ate and slept and with the first rays of the new day, bitter cold but with a late sun warming the earth gradually, they separated. Jules was going to spend the day with Doctor Baird.

Seth wanted to see the girl again. Black Horse owed him that much and more. He listened to what Seth proposed and made a long face before he answered.

"If I bring this girl to you here in my lodge, I can do that only once. Plume must not know she sees you here.

76

You will tell her that. I do not like this. It is not good."

Seth stood adamantly, waiting. When Black Horse saw that he wouldn't change his request, he arose with an uneasy, grim look, and went out. Seth squatted by the fire-hole and waited. His heart was pounding erratically. It would endanger the girl, forcing a meeting like this, but on the other hand the passage of the days would allow Black Horse's gratitude to grow stale, too.

He looked up when she came into the lodge ahead of Black Horse, who stood in the doorway for a moment, then stepped back outside. His dark face was working with tension. Seth understood his predicament, if he didn't particularly sympathise with it. He stood up. The girl's intense blue eyes were on him fully. She had an expression of resignation and patience he had never seen on a woman's face before. As though she were reconciled to almost anything, and waiting.

"Ma'm, I wanted to talk to you." She stood perfectly still, watching him. That made it no easier to say what he wanted to say. He fisted both hands and held them to his sides. "I have a picture of you." That wasn't right and he knew it. Scowling, he tried once more. "I talked to your father. He told me about the ambush. I—my pardner Jules and I—we came here to find you and try to get you away."

"I'm grateful, Mister Wolff, but—how can it be done? They watch me day and night. Plume has Two Stars with me all the time. And—if we could get away—where would we go?"

"Cache," Seth said grimly.

"What?"

"Hide—cache." He had a difficult time keeping his mind on the thing they were discussing. Jules had been so awfully wrong!

"Oh." She looked very solemnly at him. "Is it possible? I don't know the country." Her voice trailed off. "Have you a plan?"

77

"Only one," he said. "Remember when we saw each other first? Well, you go down there. Tell Plume's wife you want to bathe. When you see me, go across the creek and wait. When I think it's safe, I'll follow you."

Karin locked her fingers in a frightened, tight grip across her stomach. Her deep blue eyes were frozen on his face. For a long time she said nothing. In the hush of the lodge of Black Horse they seemed protected from the bedlam of the frenzied victory celebration coming to them in waves of noise—wild war-cries and shrill shrieks around the coup sticks where the luckless Flathead scalps hung. Into that enchanted silence she dropped three simple words.

"I am afraid."

Seth looked at her. She was beautiful, even in her filthy clothes with the over-size, Blackfoot moccasins on her feet. "Do you want to stay here until spring? We can do that. It would be wiser, my pardner thinks."

Very slowly she shook her head. "I don't think so."

"Does Plume beat you?" he asked, half-unwillingly.

She shook her head. "No. He only grabs me by the hair when he wants me to do something—fetch wood or catch his horse, or build a fire. It's—well—there's no time to talk of that." She stared at him a moment longer, then said: "Why are you doing this? It will endanger the lives of your friend, my father—and you. Why?" The deep blue eyes held an intense, questioning light. It appeared to be desperately important that she should have his answer. "You could go. . . . You and your friend could save yourselves now. Yet you stay. I don't understand. . . ."

She waited. Seth couldn't explain, not here, not now.

"Don't try to understand. Just do like I say, if you want to try getting away."

"All right. Tomorrow then."

He watched her leave the lodge. A flash of flame reflected upwards from the ground from the big "skunk" (bonfire) the Blackfeet had built, showed opaquely in the gloom of the lodge. He sat down and stretched his long legs out. Instinctively his hand went to the pouch that held the miniature. But he didn't take it out. Where was the need, when he had just seen and spoken with the reality?

He was still sitting there when Black Horse came into the tipi and stood at the flap, looking through the tipi and stood at the flap, looking through the darkness at him. "You are my brother. I am your friend. Plume will kill her if he knows she has been in the lodge of Black Horse. He will lose much prestige."

Seth nodded and got to his feet. "I go now."

But Black Horse shook his head. "No. The people are celebrating our victory. You must go among them. I will tell of your valour. They will like that."

"Plume won't," Seth said in English.

Black Horse went around the fire-hole and said nothing while he tugged out of his damp, filthy clothing and worried his way into a strikingly beautiful array of beaded and quilled buckskins with long fringes. Along the tied sides of his war-shirt were the small, dried scalplocks of enemies killed in battle. Seth watched the chieftain dress and was suddenly struck with his own appearance. Then he knew what a thoroughly wretched figure he must have cut to Karin Baird.

When Black Horse was finished dressing, he strode toward the door-flap. Seth went after him. Outside, the night was lighted up by the big "skunk." It was a barbaric spectacle, the gaunt lodgepoles sticking up above the hide coverings like twisted fingers erect in some macabre anguish. Seth sniffed. There was roast meat cooking somewhere close by.

"We go."

Seth shook his head. "I'll go scrape off as much of the mud as I can. Beaver Killer will come too."

He turned without another glance at the chief and struck off across the rapidly freezing slush underfoot and toward the lodge. The sounds of the ceremonial dancers would come in unpleasant explosions of savage unison. Cries that came from deep within powerful throats. He felt a mood upon him that matched every bit of the ferocity that was loose in the night. He was thinking about Plume giving orders to Karin.

Jules looked up when Seth entered. He had cleaned his buckskins until they were even cleaner than before the fight. The smell of their drying was in the lodge. "You been to the dance, Seth?"

"No. I talked Black Horse into getting the girl into his lodge for me to talk to."

Jules's look of surprise was overshadowed by a stare of horror. He watched the younger man peel off his hunting shirt and breeches, hunker by the fire and systematically go to work rubbing off the dried, caked filth. "That wasn't a wise thing to do."

Seth frowned at the stiff hide under his hands. "Jules, she's ready to make a run for it."

"An' what of 'er daddy? Seth, you'll be the death of that man. He couldn't pull a green hide off'n a pole. You know that."

"He won't have to. Neither will you. Jules, if we wait for spring she'll be dead. Y'ought to see her face. She's not getting enough to eat."

"But she will now, Seth," Jules said patiently. "We killed plenty of buffalo. She'll get her share."

"Not from Plume," Seth said, quietly savage. He turned the hunting shirt over and went to work on the other side with the flat side of his skinning knife.

Jules squatted by the fire-hole. His dark, sombre eyes were on the younger man's quick moving fingers and the even, stropping sweep of the knife against the caked dirt. "How are you goin' to work it, boy?" he asked evenly.

"I asked her if she wanted to get away, Jules. She was afraid, but she wanted to. I've got an idea. It's not strong, but it'll work I think."

"When you're endangerin' two lives, Seth, you want to be certain."

Seth's jaw muscles clamped but he went on scraping at the mud. "I'll have horses for you and Baird. I'll have 'em tied in the thicket on the far side of the creek. I'll try to get four of them, but I'll get two, sure—otherwise we won't even try it. You and the doctor'll ride."

Jules snorted. "How you goin' to get these horses? The Injuns're watchin' us day and night." Jules spat into the fire. It sizzled angrily. "An' why me ride, boy? Better you put the girl astride."

"No, Jules. I want the doctor astride so's he can run for it, but you—well—I want you to head for Pierre's Hole by way of Three Forks. Somewhere down there you'll find help. Fetch it back as fast as you can. I'll let 'em track me afoot."

Jules looked incredulous. "You're goin' to put that girl through a thing like *this*?"

"No. I'll cache her somewhere. Give her my pemmican and hide her, Jules. She'll be safe—you and the doctor'll be as safe as your horses are good. I'll pick the best of those Flathead critters."

"And you?" Jules asked with an unblinking stare.

"I'll lead those bucks a damned merry chase, Jules. You can bet your life on that." Seth finished with the hunting shirt. It was remarkably clean looking. He shrugged into it and picked up the mud-stiff trousers and attacked them with grim vigour.

"Seth," Jules said very soberly. "You're takin' a long chance. I don't mind the risk an' what happens to the doctor don't bother me. But the girl, Seth—you're makin' a wild move where she's concerned."

Seth went on scraping. There was a high flush in his face from the exertion and the proximity of the little fire. Jules lapsed into a moment's silence, then went on again with one large wag of his head.

"Have you figgered how many bucks'll be after you,

81

boy? They's about three hundred right here in this danged village. They all got horses. Figger yer odds."

"I have figured them," Seth said suddenly, "and they tally up to maybe a hundred or so. Out of that there'll be maybe half, that'll keep on my trail. Remember, Jules, by the time the warriors find out we're gone, it'll be damned close to sundown, too."

"Sure," Jules said, "but how do you figure no more'n fifty'll stay after us?"

Seth got up and pulled on his trousers and looked down at the older man. "Because you and I are going out to their damned celebration right now and dance and holler and raise hell like the rest of 'em are doing, only we're going to keep 'em dancing right up until sunup, Jules. Make 'em dance and holler and raise hell until they're ready to drop in their tracks. That's how we'll cut down the odds against us, when they take up the chase. Come on."

CHAPTER FIVE

THE Blackfeet were steeped in an extremely intricate and complicated religiosity. When they held sun-dances or victory celebrations there were both medicine-men and medicine-women galore. Mostly, the women had to do with the religious side of festivities while the men's societies (called Medicine Lodges) had to do with more earthy subjects such as propitiating Old Man (the Sun) who was their foremost deity, for success in war and the hunt.

However, the Blackfeet also worshipped lesser deities too. These were symbolised by such things as thunder, the weather, winter, so that any celebration, such as the one Seth and Jules went towards in the centre of the village, was invariably opened with the smoking of the calumet. Smoking was, among all Plains Indians, a sacred ceremony. Oaths were made and business transactions sealed with the smoking of the pipe. Celebrations were begun only after a very grave and imposing ritual in which the headman filled and lighted the pipe, then held it out, stem first, to the sun (Old Man) next to the earth (their Mother), after which the calumet was smoked for about three inhalations by the host, and passed to his left—"as the sun travels."

But all this had been complied with long before Seth and Jules got to the centre of the deafening clamour, and the screeching, howling, sidling and stomping dances were in full swing. Standing off on the fringe of the tribesmen, the two white trappers had a long look before they were noticed and acclaimed.

The Indian dancers had wet scalps dangling from coup sticks held aloft. Others were arrayed in beautiful garments that shone richly from the roaring blaze of the big "skunk." Others, the older Blackfeet, were content to sit or stand and keep up the primitive cadence of the bedlam with stamping feet or keening wails. Some of the dancers, man and woman, were wrapped tightly together within one blanket, bending low and jumping in short, constricted steps, together. The spectacle was one of complete barbarism, and yet there was a thread of drumming and rhythm that affected everyone present, including old Jules, who had lived a long time among the Indians. So long, in fact, that his origin and distant past were really obscure, like a faintly remembered dream, in his memory. He nudged Seth and bent his head low to speak.

"You'll have no trouble keepin' 'em dancin', boy. They've been at it all day now, what with buildin' the skunk an' gettin' ready. An' they're still as fresh as new flowers."

Seth didn't answer. The buck next to him turned and smiled widely, then let out a wild yell. The other Indians turned, saw Seth and Jules, and echoed the shout. Seth saw Plume on the far side of the circle. He was sitting decorously, as impassive and proud as ever. Black Horse stood up and emitted a sharp, high-pitched yell. The dancers slowed and looked over at the white men. The drums beat faster. Black Horse motioned them to him. By skirting the gathered people who hunkered around the dance-circle, they went over and squatted. Black Horse put his mouth close to Seth's ear and spoke in English.

"You dance soon. You show 'em how you killed the Flathead and got their horses."

Seth shook his head and nodded significantly toward Plume, saying nothing.

Black Horse followed Seth's glance, stared a moment at the great warrior's rigid back and splendid ceremonials, and swore in English, but nodded understanding. Plume would give his pantomime first. They settled down to watch the dancers after that, saying nothing. The time went by and Seth hoarded his energy for what he had in mind. It would be a rigorous ordeal at best. At worst it would be terribly exhausting to men who were going to flee these same people.

When the propitiating ceremonies were over and Old Man had been duly thanked and exorcised to give the Bloods more victories over their enemies, the drummers hammered out a wild crescendo, then stopped. The finale was abrupt and startling. The silence was complete. Not an Indian spoke or moved.

A full sixty seconds of this trance-like silence held, then Black Horse reached down and touched Plume's shoulder lightly. The big warrior got very slowly to his feet. He looked out over the multitude with his head thrown back and his black eyes flashing. One hand held his war-bow whilst the other clasped the blanket that was belted around his middle and thrown regally, toga-like, over his shoulder. Seth begrudgingly admitted the bearing and dignity of Plume were impressive. Then the warrior began to speak.

He told briefly what he had done and how he had come to do it. When he mentioned the Flatheads he did it with boundless scorn. Thus, by intimation, he was telling his people in effect that his own feat had been nothing out of the ordinary, for the Bloods were vastly superior to the vanquished enemies anyway. And the Blackfeet loved it.

"Hou, hou."

After his short résumé, Plume then shook off his blanket and stood revealed in the beautiful golden yellow of his ceremonials. Beadwork glittered and the gaudily dyed quillwork lay even and flat, worked up into Siksika devices, including the symbols of the Horn Society, of which Plume was an exalted member.

Very majestically the big Indian then stalked out into the open circle before his tribesmen, with his bow. Seth watched with grim interest and turned to Jules with a softly spoken aside.

"Danged buzzard ought to be a play-actor."

Jules didn't answer but he nodded, and no one could deny that Plume's sense of timing and drama were perfect. He waited until the silence was deathly still again, then he leaped into the air and let out a wild yell. This was the signal for the drums to start. They did, with a crashing, spine-tingling dirge that was like unexpected thunder. Some deep and dark instinct stirred in the heart of all who heard it.

Then Plume went through his pantomime with increasing frenzy up until he swung his bow with a terrible scream and struck an imaginary Flathead across the face with it. Seth took that culminating moment to sneak a quick look at Black Horse's profile. The chieftain was sitting as rigidly as a rock, but he wasn't watching Plume. He was looking steadily at the Bloods around the fire. Bitterness and hatred showed in equal parts in his face.

The Blackfeet around the "skunk" let out a simultaneous roar of acclaim as Plume turned and faced them. His chest was heaving from the strenuous labour. He threw back his head and posed—and Jules swore under his breath at the over-acting of the warrior.

Seth turned and winked. "You go next, Jules. Your's'll be easy. Just lie there nice an' warm by the 'skunk' an' make out you're firin' your rifle at Flatheads." He grinned when he said it and the older man's expression of rancour towards Plume softened. Turned into a bleak old smile that was as rueful as the shake of the head that went with it.

"You'll see no play-actin' like that fool done, boy. I ain't out to make myself chief of nothin' but a long life."

Black Horse turned at the sound of Jules's voice and looked at them both. Seth grunted and said that Plume was a great warrior. A strong-heart. He wasn't looking at Black Horse when he said it, and that was no accident either.

Plume went back to his place without so much as glancing up where the others sat. The drums kept up their throbbing rumble and a dancer of the Horn Society got up and went into a ceremonial dance of his society, indicating how great Plume his brother was, and how great the Horn Society was. This dance included enough of Plume's pantomime so that the people understood what was intended, and also the traditional movements of the Horns.

Seth watched with a little frown, then he bent toward Black Horse and spoke in rapid English. "Your dance will be laughed at. You make a big charge across the circle, then fall down within sight of the Flatheads. Your people will laugh. Plume's dance was a victory dance." He was close enough to Black Horse to see the deepening colour of the bronzed face; the vicious set of the jaw and the warning constriction of the jaw muscles.

He didn't wait for Black Horse to explode, which he knew the Blood chieftain would do under more derisive prompting. "Black Horse, listen. Only three of us know what happened. Jules and I will say nothing. You act out my coups. You kill the Flathead when they first charge up. You make the long crawl around to their horses. You bring their horses back and stampede them and kill that Flathead who ran up the hill."

Seth's words may have been spoken too rapidly for the Blood to understand them thoroughly, but that he got the drift was instantly apparent. He swung his head in a swift, violent gesture and glared at Seth. The blackness of his eyes was heightened by the fire; it reflected off their wetness.

"You are a snake."

Seth didn't lower his glance a bit. "No. You are a fool. Plume has a great coup. He has other great coups. He has the doctor and the girl alive. They are among the people always. They keep his name and prowess before them always; every day. Now, he has this other coup against the Flatheads. You are making a bad showing. You are in a bad spot."

Black Horse's face was shiny with sweat. He didn't blink an eye during the long moments of his regard of Seth. "You gave me your coup," he said.

Seth nodded. "Then act like it is yours. Don't act like I gave it to you. Act like you won it. Jules—Beaver-Killer —and I are the only ones who know. This is our secret."

"All right," Black Horse said suddenly with an infinitesimal nod, "but why do you do this?"

Seth said it softly and adamantly. He didn't particularly enjoy doing such a thing to Black Horse, but he was playing a game that included the life of Karin Baird among the stakes. "For your help in getting four of the best horses in the horse-herd."

Black Horse blinked in bewilderment. "Four?"

"Yes. One for me. One for Beaver Killer. One for the white medicine man. One for the girl."

Black Horse's grunt was throttled with considerable effort but the astonishment in his glance wasn't hidden at all. Seth knew from his previous try, that Black Horse couldn't be pushed into actually helping them escape. He had balked at that before and would be just as stubborn now. There was only one way to appeal to the chief. He had just done it. By showing him how he could salvage his honour and prestige before the people of his band. There was only one other argument in favour of his scheme left. He used it now.

"Black Horse, Plume is a great warrior. He is a proud and mighty Blood. If his prisoners are stolen from under his nose, the people will laugh at him for being unable to protect his own coups. Tie four horses across the creek at dawn, after the celebration. Let no one see you, and I will make Plume a fool in the eyes of his tribesmen."

The pulsating of the Blackfoot drums was a sinister background for the long glance the white man and the Blackfoot chieftain exchanged. Neither moved nor flickered an eyelash in the stare they held. Seth's heart was pounding. He had played every card in his hand. If Black Horse refused, there would be no chance at all of escaping the Blood village. Should the tribal loyalty triumph over the Blackfoot's hatred and fear of Plume's ascendancy, he would tell in council what Seth had proposed. If they weren't all killed outright as a result, at least their chances of escaping before spring—if then— would be voided. The loose captivity they lived under now would be done away with in favour of constant watchfulness.

Seth knew all this. It was foremost in his mind while he waited for Black Horse's decision. The Indian finally turned his head very slowly away from the white man. At that precise moment the wild dance of the Horn Society's representative ended with a harsh scream from the cross-legged watchers. The same prolonged silence settled again. A Kit-Fox warrior then arose in full warrior regalia. His buckskin shirt, in true Blackfoot style, was split down both sides under the arms and tied together with three thongs. His leggings were stained bright yellow and painted with black horizontal stripes. They were held up by being tied to his belt, and the open front and rear were covered by a red breechcloth. He wore a buffalo-horn bonnet of some white fur. Through each tip of the buffalo horns was pulled a short length of tanned thong from which dangled two or three small orange feathers.

The warrior held out both hands directly in front of him, arms stiff, palms downward. The silence lengthened before he spoke. Then, in a ringingly deep voice the buck began his oration by citing past coups of the band's leader, Black Horse. He went on from fights to successful horse stealing expeditions against the Dakotas, the Crows, the Flatheads and Snakes, and wound it all up with a thunderous stomp of one moccasined foot and a sharp demand that their chieftain now come forward and show the people how powerful his medicine was against the recently vanquished Flathead hunters.

Seth was holding himself tightly. His hands were locked in a tight grip in his lap. He dared not lean over and talk to Black Horse again.

The anxiety was terrible.

His last chance slipped away when Black Horse stood up and cast aside his blanket with a manly flourish, and stood like a statue, looking over the head of Plume and the others on his side of the fire, toward the Kit-Fox brave. They faced each other for a moment, then the Kit-Fox in the buffalo-horn bonnet threw back his head and raised the yell. It was immediately taken up by the other Indians. Seth noted that here and there among the assemblage, some Bloods sat in silence, staring stony-faced, straight ahead. He deduced that these were the followers of Plume.

Then Black Horse went forward into the circle and Seth turned to Jules. "I told him you and I'd never tell what happened with the Flatheads if he'd give us four strong horses and a chance to escape."

"If you'd let him count your coup he might have done it."

"I told him that. Said for him to act out what I did. The surround and all the rest." Seth studied the calm and thoughtful face of old Jules. The older man watched Black Horse stand before his people in haughty silence, disdaining to give the résumé first. His black eyes were fastened to the big chieftain when he spoke aside to Seth.

"Did he answer you?"

"No."

"Then set back," Jules said. "They're a coyote bunch at best. You've tossed the fat in the fire anyway, boy. Either way we've got to make medicine now. If he tells the council what you offered him, they'll tell Plume, and that means the girl'll get her skull split. And if he don't tell 'em—why—he'll have us watched like so many creepin' enemies in the grass." The look Jules turned towards Seth was a saturnine smile. "All right, boy. You wanted to fetch it to a head. Now you've done her. If you was a prayin' man, I'd say pray." He looked back at the dense crowd across from them, and shrugged. "Wish I was close enough to that skunk to send up a hair-smoke of prayer for all of us."

Seth frowned. The drums were starting again. He ignored them and looked at Jules's profile. "Listen, Jules. Baird's in the crowd somewhere. When I do my dance, wander around looking for him."

Jules looked around. "Why?"

"Tell him to make his way to the creek, cross it and wait over there at dawn. Tell him I'll be over there somewhere, with as many horses as I can get—for him to look for me. Tell him if he misses me—misses us, I mean—he'll be dead before sundown tomorrow evening."

Jules searched Seth's face for a long time. The drums were building up to their thunderous tempo slowly. "You're certain to try it then?" Seth nodded curtly. Jules's face softened, strangely, and he nodded and looked away again. "All right. I'll hunt him up an' tell him. How about the girl? You'll take care of that?"

"Yeh. But I'll wait until the general dance starts after all the coup dances."

"Well," Jules said slowly, "you'll find her with Plume's Sits-Beside-Him-Woman. I seen 'em together an hour or so ago, across the way there."

After that, talk was impossible. The drums were making tremours rumble under the ground so that every squatting person could feel them come up along their spines and add to the measure of primitive savagery in their hearts and souls.

Seth watched Black Horse go through the initial gyrations of the buffalo hunt he and the two white men had started out on, then his glance drifted over the crowd. The Bloods were watching their chieftain closely. The looks among them were intent, ranging from pride to anticipation. Among the hundreds of dark faces, some sitting, some standing, all clothed in their very best ceremonials, were many warriors. Seth took particular notice of their expressions, and deduced from them that Plume, for all his vaunted greatness, had only a small number of adherents as yet to his clique.

Then he saw Karin Baird and her father. They were a little apart; the doctor's face showed obvious anguish and fear. The girl was turning away from his glance when her eyes crossed with the steady look of Seth.

It was as though a message passed between them. He could feel the tightness growing in his chest. Frantically, he sought around for a way to let her know he wanted to talk to her, but there was no way to signal in front of all those Indians, some of whom he knew would be watching both of them. He contented himself with a small smile that was meant to convey encouragement to her, then Jules was brushing his hand over Seth's sleeve and bending toward him with a wan little grin of his own.

"There's yer answer, boy. There; watch 'im."

Seth dropped his glance to Black Horse. The Blood chieftain was simulating firing his war-bow at invisible Flatheads. Every once in a while he would look down, as though anxious for the safety of unseen companions. Then, very carefully, with exaggerated looks about him and behind, Black Horse began bellying over the ground in a large circle. He was pantomiming the surround Seth had made, preparatory to reaching and stampeding the Flathead horse-herd. There was no doubt about it, Black Horse was enacting Seth's coups as though they were his own.

Jules puckered his mouth up into a silent whistle, and sighed.

"You got him where he had to do it, boy. That was damned clever. I hope the rest of your scheme's just half as good."

"I do too," Seth said softly but fervently, then he continued to watch the dance.

Black Horse finally leapt up with a wild shout and acted out the driving of horses ahead of him. He paused only once more, and that was to fire his bow at another imaginary Flathead, then he sidled back with stomping steps to where Seth and Jules were supposedly lying, helped each on to a horse and led them back toward the Blackfoot village.

When the dance was almost over and the Indians were rocking exultantly, waiting for the drums to stop so they could voice their wholehearted approval and affection for their leader, Seth turned his head a little and looked down where Plume was sitting. The warrior was as stiffly erect as a ramrod. His profile, lighted by the dancing, red blaze, was frozen into a mask of impassiveness that didn't quite hide the seething fury beneath. Seth was so fascinated by the terrible look on Plume's face that when Jules's fingers brushed over his arm again, he gave a slight start.

"Baird's girl is lookin' at you. I got a notion it'll be easier for me to see her while you're givin' your dance, than for you to do it later, while I'm out there. Anyway, I'll try it. What do you want me to tell her; same as her daddy?"

Seth nodded. "I spoke to her about it already, but tell her about the horses."

"Yeh. Anythin' else?"

"Nothing. If you get a chance t'tell her that, you'll be lucky. The other'll save."

Jules's glance held speculatively to Seth's face until the younger man flushed, then the little grin came back. "I'll tell 'er, Seth," he said. "You'd better make Black Horse spit it out, too. He can't go back on his dance an' he knows it—but make damned sure those're the best critters they got, for I've no stomach for tryin' to outrun a herd of blood-eyed Blackfeet on a weak horse. Tell him if they ain't the best horses, an' we git took alive, he'd best make tracks for Fort McKenzie 'cause his band'll just string his innards around the bushes like old rope."

"He'll keep his word," Seth said. "Hell, he *has* to, after that dance."

Jules nodded grimly and straightened up. The drums beat up into their wild crescendo again, then stopped. The big silence came again. Black Horse walked past Plume on his way to his place beside Seth. Neither Blood warrior looked at the other. Seth studiously avoided the chief until another warrior—this one with his face painted a grotesque white through the over-application of dampened ash and bone-chalk—stood up and began a wavering, falsetto recitation of the deeds of the white man called Medicine Walker. Then Seth grunted and spoke without looking at Black Horse. The chief listened the same way, with his eyes fixed on the Indian warrior across the circle from them.

"Tie the four horses across the bathing creek. Up where the little boys bathe. Pick only the best horses. You are my brother. I will show my gratitude."

"How?" Grunted the Blood.

Seth answered softly. "In many ways. As your always-friend. As the always-friend of your band."

"You have asked all the favours. I have given to you. All right. We are brothers. Now *I* ask."

"Ask," Seth said.

"Two things. You do not let them take you alive. You do not let them take Beaver Killer or the white medicine-man or the female alive. I will get the best horses. You must never tell any white men of this. You are my brother. This will be forever our secret. I will never tell it. You will never tell it."

"Hou," Seth said. "What is the other thing you want? You have asked two already."

"No," Black Horse said vehemently. "The secret is the same. If you don't let them take you alive it is the same thing."

"All right. What else?"

94

"Plume will chase you. He will follow you the hardest. He will avenge his strong-heart. He has to. I want you to kill him. I want you to do that above everything else. I want you to say you will kill Plume."

Seth held his silence for a moment, then nodded. "I will kill Plume if I can. I will try hard. Beyond that I cannot say."

"I am satisfied," Black Horse said.

Seth considered reiterating what Jules had grimly suggested he say to the chief, but he decided against it. There was no need to threaten the chief. It was also very possible that, being threatened, Black Horse might be angered. It was better left alone; as it was.

The chalk-faced Blood, gotten up to indicate that he was the pipe-talker for Seth and Jules, hence the whitened face, was winding up his harangue. Knowing the last time he would have for speaking aside to Black Horse was at hand, Seth spoke once more, bluntly and rapidly.

"When the dancing is at its height, go tie the horses. We will try to get away about dawn. When we are no longer here, make your people dance, Black Horse. Make them dance as long as you can. We need a long start."

The silence settled again and Seth stood up. The great circle of dark eyes and shiny faces were turned toward him. He knew that those people had worked all day long without stopping, preparing for this rarest of all victory celebrations, a winter triumph over enemies. A victory dance was unheard of in the time of the Long Sleep when men, like animals and plants, were torpid with stiff marrow in their bones and little desire to be out in the bitter weather.

He went forward, shot a fast, sidling glance over the Indians around Karin, and saw Jules slouching among them, watching Seth as though absorbed with the prospect. Then he very elaborately and slowly began enacting the proposed buffalo hunt by peering into a supposedly empty pouch, then looking up into the sky and down at the earth. He closed his eyes tightly and made a medicine sign, depicting a strong hunter seeking a medicine-vision. After that he opened his eyes wide and leapt into the air. The Indians howled appreciatively. The drums crashed into life again and Seth's dance was on.

He used the same sidling, stamping, hell-and-toe step Black Horse and Plume had used. With lavish flourishes that pleased the assembled Bloods greatly, and throwing himself into his part like a veteran dancer, Seth acted out the entire part Black Horse had actually played in the abortive hunt, but depicting Black Horse's part as though he, himself, had been temporarily knocked senseless when the horse had been shot out from under him.

He covered his eyes when indicating how Black Horse had crept away alone to surround the Flatheads and get their horses. He struck his chest mightily to indicate the strong-heart of the great Blood chieftain when he had been dragged to safety, unconscious, and he left no doubt in any Blood's mind about his own negligible part in the victory.

The Indians were rigid with concentrated interest until Seth gave the final mighty leap that culminated his pantomime, then they broke into cheers and laughter. He threw them a smile, scorning the accepted hauteur of a dancer when his enactment was over, and strolled back to his place. Breathing heavily from the exertion, he made no answer when Black Horse grunted aside to him.

"Damn good. *Heap* damn good."

The chalk-faced warrior stood again. His gestures indicated Jules's part in the recent battle. Seth sought his pardner's face among the Indians around Karin and didn't find it. Then he saw Jules coming out into the circle from another direction and wisely looked for Doctor Baird. He saw the medical man almost instantly. If Baird had shouted over the noise of the drums and told Seth that Jules had explained what they planned, it wouldn't have been any more evident than the look on the doctor's face. Baird's eyes were round and almost black-looking. His pallid features with their underlay of yellow fat were loose and flabby with fright. Seth looked away in disgust.

Jules was an old hand at Indian dancing. He went through his role as though he were a Blackfoot. The Indians smiled often but made no sound until it was over, then they shouted cheerful obscenities at Jules, who mocked Plume's and Black Horse's haughtiness afterward by striking an exaggerated pose of tremendous and ludicrous pride. The Bloods were convulsed. They shouted and hooted until Jules threw them a careless wave and went back into the crowd again, to become lost in the general movement of all the people, who now got to their feet and stomped circulation into their limbs preparatory to joining in the general scalp dance that was to follow. Seth got up seconds after Black Horse did. He brushed past the stalwart chieftain and went down among the Indians.

Chance brought Seth and Plume face to face when the dancers started to shriek and move. The black eyes of the Blood-Blackfoot were like burning oil. He drew back his lips and ground out a fierce grunt. He would have cursed Seth roundly, the white man knew, except for the fact that no Plains Indian language had any profane words at all, and Plume apparently knew no English words that were appropriate. Hence the murderous grunt.

Seth ignored the buck and started to dance by when Plume leaned over and spoke harshly into his face, in Siksika. "You have a forked tongue. Black Horse's heart is in the mud. *You* had no blood in your hair when you rode back to the people. Black Horse did have. *He* was knocked senseless and *you* dragged him to safety. You both lied to the people. He took your coups."

Seth's muscles tightened up instinctively, but he said nothing. Just threw the big Blood a cold look and danced on past. He didn't look as though he was enjoying the dance after the encounter with Plume, and he wasn't. Not until he saw Karin Baird being pushed along ahead of Plume's wife, making awkward attempts to keep step with the lurching, whirling, stomping and jumping Blackfeet. Then he danced harder, faster, until he had jostled his way over beside the girl and spoke to her in a quick, harsh way.

"Did Jules tell you about the horses?"

She nodded, her intensely blue eyes holding to his face with a sort of frantic desperation. But she didn't speak. Didn't get a chance to. Plume's angry-eyed squaw slammed herself in between them with a fierce scream of rage.

Seth instantly moved sideways, but the damage had been done. The dancers nearest them stopped and stared. The drummers faltered in their timing and a burly shoulder brushed past Seth so that he was pushed off balance a little. By the time he had regained his footing, Plume was glaring at him with a face twisted and terrible in its rage.

Without speaking to any of them, the warrior seized her with a broad, fiercely-strong hand. He went through the little throng of startled watchers dragging her behind him like a broken doll. There was a threatening fury in his firelit face.

Seth was rooted to the ground for just a split second. Then he turned away from them and after an elaborate expectoration in the direction of the retreating warrior, grimaced and swung out into a dance so wild and abandoned the Blackfeet were instantly caught up in its tempo.

Through the long chill of the small hours the Indians danced. A few would drift off where the huge slabs of meat were being cooked in trenches, eat their fill, drink snow-water, then come back to dance some more. Once, Jules swung in beside the younger man. His grin was fixed and terribly forced-looking.

"Gawd a'mighty, Seth. I figgered our time'd comed

98

when I seen that. I got respect for you boy. I got more respect than I ever had afore for a man. You done right. Too much to lose now. He's back—must 'a just kicked her a little. He's dancin' yonder again."

Seth hadn't lifted his head nor stopped dancing since it had happened. Now he did and the wolfishness in his glance startled Jules. He spoke in English, harshly and quickly. "Jules, I'm going to kill the critter for that. I'm going to gut him like a snowbird." That was all he said. He dropped his head and whirled as madly as any Blood Indian in the vast throng. But Jules hadn't said all he wanted to, so he kept close.

"I told 'em both, boy. They're ready. The doctor—I don't know—not much to 'im."

Seth spoke without even raising his head. "If he can't keep up with you, Jules, let the damned Injuns have him. T'hell with a man'd lead his daughter into a thing like this."

Jules wisely said no more. He could see the uncontrollable rage that held Seth in its grip. Inwardly, Jules made a promise too. If he was afforded just one fleeting shot at Plume, the Indian would be a long time dying, but he would die. For old Jules knew a lot of ways to kill a man that weren't sudden.

Black Horse danced until the bedlam was at its height, then he went among the hungry Bloods around the meat-pits and gorged himself in true Indian style. Ate until his stomach was distended and he was totally uncomfortable. Seth watched him more than he watched Jules or Plume or any of the other dancers, but there were too many people. At least five hundred. More, counting the little bucks and squaws-to-be, who yelled and squealed among the dancers, along with their half-wild dogs.

These added to the excitement by frequently tripping an adult, causing much hilarity and many villainous kicks at the dogs and children that never quite connected.

The pageantry of it all didn't impress Doctor Baird, Seth, Jules, or the girl who lay with her face in the damp, frozen grass. Days of unending toil, nights without sleep, insufficient food and many beatings, to culminate in this —a bruised, aching body begging the iron-hard ground to hide it, to shelter it, so that it might gather enough strength for the escape attempt next day. And please, please—not to let Plume be angry with her again. . . .

A source of considerable amusement among the dancers was the medical-man. Despite his repeated and obviously sincere efforts to comply with the tickling knife-point of Plume, he couldn't catch the rhythm of the Blackfoot dance. His best efforts were convulsively funny to the Indians. Seth felt a pang of pity for him, especially since Plume's knife drew blood through the thin and tattered clothing of the white man every time the warrior encouraged Doctor Baird with its point. But both he and Jules entered into the laughter, yet once, when Baird looked frantically over at them, his glassy stare was more livid with desperation than reproach.

Seth's anger congealed into a solid, icy determination. As he flung through the dance he considered killing Plume before they fled the camp, but cast the idea aside because it would be necessary to do it by stealth, and knifing the big warrior in his sleep wasn't what Seth wanted at all. Calmer reflection indicated it would be senseless—downright idiotic to court disaster in the face of what lay ahead for them.

When the dancers would slacken off in their frenzied leaps and shouts, Seth would drive them to new efforts with a show of endurance that stung the Bloods to strive and excel the white man. Jules was sitting among the oldsters along the sidelines holding up a great, dripping slice of meat. He flagged Seth with it, grinning from ear to ear. Seth went over dripping perspiration, his clothes dark with it, and dropped down beside the old trapper

"You're doin' right well, boy," Jules said, holding the

100

haunch out for Seth to slice off a slab of it. "If you don't fall down dead afore dawn, we might be able to keep 'em a-goin'. You seen Black Horse lately?"

Seth looked among the crowd and shook his head. His heart was pounding like the drums, only faster. He shrugged. "They're packed together like pine needles, Jules. You couldn't see him if he was ten feet in front of you."

Jules grunted and moved his legs to keep the stiffness out. The ground was very cold on the fringes of the dancing circle, away from the fire. "Allus like to eat a big supper when it might by my last," he said. "I filled my pouch with pemmican from what the squaws gave me."

"Good. We'll need it."

Jules flicked loose the pucker-string holding his parfleche to his belt. "Here. You put on mine an' I'll go fill yours. That way we'll have enough for *them*, too."

Seth made the exchange, knotted Jules's pouch on to his belt and felt the added weight of it. He was watching the dancers and sucking in great lungfuls of cold night air.

"You see Baird a-tryin' to dance? Plume's a blood-thirsty cuss. I hope he follers after me 'stead of you and the girl. I like to make bucks like him eat crow."

The possibility had never occurred to Seth that the warrior he hated with such solid intensity might not follow his tracks. He frowned in thought, then brightened again. "I'll get him on my tracks, Jules. I want him worse than you do."

"I reckon," Jules said laconically, biting out more meat and wiping away the grease with his sleeve. He peered up at Seth squintingly. "You up to keepin' 'em hoppin' another two, three hours? It'll take that long, boy. Winter dawns come late, you know."

"I'll keep them dancing, Jules. You get the pemmican and let me know if you see Black Horse anywhere. One of us'll have to slip away directly and see if he's tied the horses across the creek. When we're sure, we'll go."

Seth was standing, bending his legs, flexing them when Jules got up still clutching his big piece of meat. "I'll check on the horses, Seth," he said. "I'm plumb danced out. You keep 'em dancin' an' leave the horses to me. If I find 'em over there, I'll let you know."

"Let the others know first, Jules. Get them to run for it before we do. Tell 'em to wait for us but to get astride and be ready."

"Yeh." Jules grunted. His little black eyes were shining with excitement as Seth moved among the dancers again.

CHAPTER SIX

WHILE the Siksika attached considerable importance to eagle feathers as did all other Plains Indians, they attached even greater value to white weasel skins as decorations. These small, luxurious skins were carefully tanned and attached to their ceremonial clothing. Thus it was that the primitive adornment of the dancers Seth moved amongst had great quantities of these little white skins flouncing and jouncing and adding to the general appearance of savageness that characterised the entire great mass of people.

For the most part the people danced out of sheer exuberance, but in time even their indomitable stamina began to fail a little and more and more warriors found places among the sitting circle of older men and women. These Seth constantly harangued. The perspiration dripped from his nose in the *danse macabre*, and his eyes shone like dull metal, but he had little trouble taunting the Bloods back into the revelry. While they could laugh off a similar taunt by a fellow Blood, they were honour-bound to accept what amounted to a challenge from a white man.

Into the swaying, incohesive mass that lurched and stomped, leapt and shrieked and shuffled the cold bit deeper, until the only place of warmth was up next to the "skunk." There, the dancers seemed to gravitate until they were packed too densely to do more than howl and sway a little. Seth managed to break that up only by repeatedly dancing through them time after time, until the dancers were shamed away from the heat. He seemed to be inexhaustible. The Indians commented upon it among themselves and the older men wagged their heads and spoke behind their turkey-wing fans to one another.

"Medicine-Walker will sleep all day after this."

"He will be stiff in the muscles and rickety in the joints."

"Hou. He is a great dancer just the same."

"Hou. Hou."

And Seth only paused in his gyrations to smile into the watching faces, give a mighty jump and a wild leap and settle down to more stomping and posturing.

He had the admiration of most of the Bloods. But there were many, like Plume, who had an ingrained hatred of all whites. To these, Seth's stamina was more of a challenge than to the others. Many laughed and gestured him away in their exhaustion, but the grim visaged, rock-hearted warriors who took Seth's endurance as a personal issue, rocked back into the dance and kept pace with him. These, though, rarely shouted or showed any of the spontaneous exuberance they had hours before. They were dancing only to prove to themselves and the other Bloods that no white man could out-last them.

And Seth kept it up until he caught a glimpse of Black Horse among the distant dancers. Then he began working his way through the throng of people with renewed vigour until they moved aside, crying out encouragement, and tried to follow his wild example. Close enough, Seth stared fixedly at the chieftain. Black Horse all but ignored him. Only once did he look straight at the white trapper, and that was when he threw back his head and thundered a strong-heart Blood battle cry and wound it up with little barks that said "yes, yes, yes," in shrill staccato yelps. Then Seth let the crowd of dancers jostle him away from the leader and swirl him here and there among the sweating Indians.

He found Jules quite by accident. Consumed with a maddening thirst, Seth stooped to dip up a drink from a snow-water filled buffalo paunch, using the scraped horn cup that was thrust at him by a grinning, toothless old crone. And there was Jules staring at him without a smile, from the purple shadows beyond the old squaw's squatting place. Seth drank several times, deeply, watching Jules's face over the rim of the horn cup. And Jules nodded once as he moved around the sitting old woman and held out his hand for the cup. Seth handed it over, rinsed his mouth and spat. Jules dipped out water, lifted it and drank, then looked at the cup and nodded his head towards it.

"They're o'er there tied up, boy. Good critters. I sent old puss-gut an' his girl over there a few minutes gone. You'll have to make it quick now. I'm goin' fer our guns. Meet you o'er there."

Seth cocked his head at the cup and touched it with his fingers. The effect was simple. They appeared to be discussing the quality of the water. "Hurry, Jules. I'll be down there as soon as I dance twice more around the fire and stir up those bucks that've dropped out, once more."

Jules turned and clapped Seth on the back and they both laughed. Then Seth howled a weird cry that was a Flathead warrior's war chant and went jumping back into the dance. The Bloods took up the cry until others among them roared back the defiant Blackfoot war chants, and the dance surged to another crescendo of weaving, screaming and earth-stomping.

Seth had no trouble inciting the warriors to dance that last time. He would dance among them, chopping the air with his chin and emitting more Flathead war cries. The bucks would instantly take up the challenge, leap up and let out a resounding Blood war-cry and stamp after him.

He led them among the other dancers until the huge crowd of Indians was locked in another paroxysm of motion. Then he began to dance away from them until he was among the squaws, some of whom called out encouragement to him and laughed uproariously.

He waved with an exhausted grin, and pushed through them. The night beyond the excited circle and the blazing fire was even colder than he had anticipated. Making his legs move slowly for a change, he ambled clear of the village, squatted once to skyline the land ahead for obstacles, human or otherwise; then he stood up, cast a glance behind him and struck out in a lazy jog for the creek.

The sudden emergence of a tall gaunt figure right in his path gave him no time to sidestep. Swinging out with a savage fist, he felled the other even as he recognised her. Plume's Sits-Beside-Him-Woman! With a gasp of dismay, he drew back; then he stooped quickly, stripped off the woman's beaded ceremonial dress, cast a final glance at the unconscious squaw and turned and ran with all his strength.

The willows loomed up first, then, just beyond, the sullen grey lustre of the creek shone. He didn't stop nor hesitate but plunged right into the icy water and splashed across it with constricted breath. The shock was almost paralysing to his over-heated body. Emerging upon the other side he saw a man running toward him with two long-rifles, one in each fist. He dropped flat but knew who it was even as he did so.

"Jules?"

"Yeh. Here." Jules thrust out Seth's gun, powder-horn and shot pouch. "They're over yonder a bit. Come on an' hurry, boy."

Following the old trapper Seth ran on legs that seemed turning to moss. There was no sense of feeling any longer, in most of his body. Aware of the dangerous numbness that presaged complete exhaustion, he locked his jaws and stayed in Jules's tracks until the ghostly silhouettes of mounted riders sprang out of the blackness at him. Then he slowed to a panting walk, glancing up into the agonised and terror stricken blobs of pale, sickly white, that were the faces of Doctor Baird and Karin.

Jules was shoving a grass rein into his hand. "Get up, boy. Get up an' God favour you. I'll take him," with a

106

brusque jerk of his dark head toward the doctor, "an' ride like hell for Three Forks. If I don't rouse no help there, I'll head south for Pierre's Hole. I'll keep a-goin' until I roust up some help somewhere, if I got to fetch back Gabe's Snakes to clean out the varmints. Which way you headin'?"

"We'll make a big sashay, Jules. Leave a lot of tracks and do a lot of doublin' around, then we'll head after you. If we aren't around when you start back, check Three Forks an' Pierre's Hole for us. We'll be around that country somewhere."

Jules cut off the beginning of something Doctor Baird was going to say, with a brusque swear word. "Come on, medicine-man," he said. "Hang on for your danged life —and ride!"

Seth saw the doctor's startled face once, head-on, then the man's horse leapt out under a blow from Jules's rifle butt and the two of them went thundering off across the freezing ground. Seth turned towards Karin, saw the dried blood on the front of her dress and thought of something. Holding out the beautifully beaded, chalky-white ceremonial dress of Plume's wife, he smiled over at her.

"Here. Don't put it on now, we haven't time, but keep it. When we can spare a few minutes you can dress up in it. It's buckskin and'll keep you a heap warmer'n what you've got on. Now, Karin—don't talk. Just hang on and follow me. No matter how tired you get, recall that Plume's back there, and a couple hundred other bucks that'll gut you if you fall behind and get caught. You'll never be a Blackfoot prisoner again. They'll kill you next time. Remember that, Karin—and stay with me."

He turned his horse and struck out. The night was unbelievably black. He had to reconstruct what he recalled of Moon Prairie from his memory, and trust in the fabulous luck that had allowed them all to be mounted, which is more than he'd really hoped for or expected to have happen.

The first three hours they rode in a sweeping arc around the northern end of the valley, above and then south-west a little, and finally due south. And they didn't ride hard at all, not then. That came later when the dawn was beginning to force a slit of weak light between the grey overcast and the mountains. Then Seth lifted his horse into a long-legged, sloppy kind of a lope, and held him to it. The animal seemed strong enough, which was surprising, considering what he'd been living on since the grass had gone. He pointed his ears forward and never wavered.

Seth looked back often at Karin. The girl's eyes were violet pools in a face of pinched features and blue lips. When he had made the little crooked valley between the Belts, he reined up and waited for her. "You can rest a few minutes. I'm going atop that ridge over yonder and see if they're after us yet." He slid down and handed her the single rein of his bridle. When their hands touched, he looked up at her swiftly. She was like ice. "You'd better slip that dress on over your other clothes."

She nodded at him. He noticed how tightly she was holding her jaws together, then he turned and trotted toward a long, rippling ridge that was barren of brush and slippery underfoot with the warm air that was washing over it after the night's frost.

Up where he could see, an icy finger of wind curled around him fleetingly, then reluctantly let go and passed by. He stood facing over their backtrail. The distances were immeasurably vast. It took a long time to catch movement and then he had to fix each landmark in his mind and wait. But there was no pursuit visible so far as he could tell. Going back down toward the horses and the girl, he looked over at her. She had donned Plume's wife's beaded dress. Except for being too long, it fitted her very well. Better, in fact, than it had its original owner. He smiled up at her, trying to look encouraging.

"You feel all right?"

She nodded impassively. He untied his parfleche pouch and handed it up. "Here. Eat some of this as you ride. It doesn't have much of a taste if you aren't used to it, but it'll sure keep you alive."

She took the sack without meeting his glance. "I hope so," she said through locked teeth, then she forced a smile that was so palpably forced that she had the good sense not to try and hold it. He frowned at her.

"You feel all right?"

"We'd better ride," she said, looking past him at the jumbled, rugged spires that jutted all around them, on both sides and ahead.

He turned then, went back to his horse, vaulted onto its back and tugged it around. They were going due south and he held to that course until he saw the willows of a creek. Then he rode over to them, leaned and pushed through, turned directly into the creek and rode his horse down the middle of it. Karin followed without showing surprise or wonder. He tried to catch a glimpse of her face but couldn't. She kept her head down so that all he saw was the wealth of her thick hair, and that reminded him of Plume. He twisted forward on the horse and kept him floundering in the mud and slippery rocks for another mile, then reined out and headed into the broken, serrated, rugged country west of them.

They kept going that way until he saw a streamer of smoke rising into the late daylight. He grunted in surprise, reined left and right along their route until he saw a grassy south slope where the heat, what there was, would always gather winter times, and slid off his horse. The ravenous animal dropped its head at once and began cropping the snow-free grass. Seth walked back and helped Karin down. She was solid and heavy. It surprised him. When she turned to face him, he got another shock; there were tears in her eyes that she hadn't quite been able to hide. troubled, he held her for a moment, then let her go.

"Don't worry, ma'm. They'll make it, I'm pretty sure."

He turned and motioned toward the matted, beaten down grass. "There. You rest there a little. I'm going to do a little scouting around." He purposefully avoided telling her of the fire he'd seen. She walked very unsteadily to where both horses were gorging themselves and sat down. The ground was dry. He felt helpless for some reason, as he looked down at her, then he swung abruptly away, taking his rifle and running a quick hand over the hatchet and knife at his belt.

The fire was west of them at least three miles. It wasn't more than a solitary, stingy little banner going straight up. Guessing it was Flathead hunters, he jogged toward it. The land was drier over here and that helped the footing. His soggy moccasins were shapeless pieces of hide that protected his feet from stones and little else.

It took a long time to get within scouting range of the cooking fire, and when he did he was lying flat on the ground with his rifle pushed out ahead of him. The visibility was too poor, however, for the lengthening shadows had kept pace with Seth's advance over the land and late evening was at hand. Cursing to himself, he wormed his way closer still—and the chance of discovery through a dislodged rock or being scented by the Indian horses, grew apace.

Finally, as close as he could get with prudence, he lay flat and worked his way up behind some dying clumps of sage, parted the brittle, wiry bushes and peered at the fire beyond. There were four Indians there, but they weren't Flatheads. They were obviously do-or-die young bucks out on a secret medicine raid, testing their medicine-visions prior to joining some large raiding party. They were the most dangerous of all fighting Indians.

Seth watched them for a long time. Each had a quiver full of arrows, a stubby little war-bow and a lance with coup feathers or scalplocks tied mid-way down the haft. They were cooking antelope meat by the simple expedient of boiling it within its own hide, which had been filled with

110

water and was sizzling and steaming within the perimeter of a cooking fire. Obviously, the Indians considered themselves so far from any possible enemy that they could risk the smoke overhead. Just as obvious, to Seth at any rate, was the fact that they didn't know the country, or they would have known that the Blackfeet used it extensively for wintering.

He studied the bucks until satisfied that they were Crows, then he flattened out and relaxed. It looked like being a long wait, and it was. The bucks talked a while after they had eaten, then they smoked. With the infinite patience of a mountain man, Seth lay perfectly still and waited until they rolled into their robes. Then he waited another long two hours before he dared work his legs under him. It wasn't the Crows that made him do that, it was the fire. It lit up their camp for six or eight feet all around. Satisfied though, at long last, Seth got up and went out into the night and circled it until he found what he was looking for. The four Crow war-horses.

They were daubed with zig-zag markings in vermilion, and two had eagle feathers braided into their foretops. All of them looked pretty well ridden down and tired. Because of that, however, Seth was able to approach them after only a minimum of manoeuvring. He led them by their war-bridles—which were also employed as hobbles—a long mile out from the Crow bivouac, then another mile south, before he dared swing up on to the largest of the four and lead them all back to the little glade where Karin Baird was sitting, her eyes as large as knots and a deathly fear in her face.

When he swung down she fought against the quiver that threatened to overcome her. He smiled, seeing the terror in her face and understanding it all right. Knowing what a terrible ordeal it must have been for her, waiting there, not knowing where she was or whether he'd ever come back or not.

"Got us some more horses." He squatted and made

hobbles out of the Crow bridles, went over and dropped beside her in the grass. "I'm sorry, Karin. I didn't reckon it'd take this long to get 'em."

She looked at the animals, dimly opalescent in the darkness. "Did you kill some more Indians?"

Taken aback, he blinked at her. "No, ma'm. I didn't have to kill these. They went to sleep and I stole their horses."

Her face was close to his when she looked back at him. "Did—you kill Plume's wife?" She was holding her skirt of soft, white buckskin in her hands tightly, looking directly at him.

He shook his head and felt irritation coming up inside himself. "No. I knocked her senseless by mistake and took off the dress. I knew you'd need it." He got up and looked at their horses. "Are you ready to ride?"

"Yes." She stood up facing him. "Seth? How much longer?"

"Longer?" He was scowling a little. It added nothing to a face already forbidding looking with its month-long straggle of beard, the dried sweat and grime of the victory dance, and the sagging fatigue that was stamped into every line, deeply. "I don't know. Does it matter? We've got to keep going until we find either Bridger's friendly Snakes —Shoshoni Indians—or white men." He shrugged. "Maybe four, five days. Maybe ten days. I don't know."

She could sense his irritation—hear it too—in spite of the darkness. She went a little closer to him. "I'm sorry. I don't mean to sound—"

"All right, ma'm," he said brusquely. "Let's ride. You can have any horse you want. We're only taking them along to make the trackers wonder. It'll draw them off Jules's tracks, and your father's."

He mounted his horse and watched her do the same thing. She did it, and twice he could see the way she gasped at the effort. Worried he turned and let the big Crow horse with the eagle feather in its foretop, strike

112

out southward in a shambling but fast, flat-footed walk.

They kept going without a stop until just before dawn. Karin had completely lost all sense of time and direction. Seth rarely looked back at her any more. Instead he rode like a man lost in thought. It was useless to look for landfalls because the land was strange to him. Nevertheless, he had to keep the thread of his trail in his mind's eye because he was deliberately backtracking, then hunting up rocky places and keeping the horses on them as long as possible.

In fact, he used every stratagem he could think of, to hide and cover up their tracks. Then, just before dawn, he struck out due south and made the dragging horses trot a while, then lope, then walk fast. He was riding to gain distance by then, satisfied with what he'd done to confuse trackers all night long.

When the grey showed once more there was a dazzling shaft of sunlight in it. He reined up and waited for the weary, head-down, Crow horse to bring Karin up to him.

She was reeling drunkenly on its back.

Startled, Seth slid down and walked back to her. She had her eyes tightly closed. There were circles of blue under each eye and her face had an ill, grey look. He reached up and touched her hand. It wasn't cold at all, and that made him all the more uneasy.

"Ma'm? Are you sick?"

She opened her eyes but they didn't focus very well on his face. "Will we be home soon?" she murmured.

"Home?"

She closed her eyes again. Her head nodded forward.

"Karin!" Seth said sharply.

The eyelids slowly crept up to reveal the violet eyes fuzzed and blank with fever.

"The stewpans," she said, "and the trunks with my clothes. . . . The freight wagon was to deliver them ahead of us." Her speech was slurred, slow, toneless. "It'll be . . . nice . . . to put on a clean dress."

113

He reached up and pulled her off the horse. Her body was burning.

"Karin," he said in an urgent voice. The sound cut through her dream of domestic comfort, of peace and normality and cleanliness. She stared at him in a moment's anxious recognition.

"Oh, Seth. I'm so sorry. I didn't ever want to let you down like this."

"It's all right, ma'm. Nobody can't help being sick. Don't you worry, I'll—"

But she no longer heard him. Her face had gone empty and slack, her body limp.

She had fainted.

He stood up and looked at the country they were passing through with a desperate glance. She couldn't go any farther. Raging with an almost irrational fury, he sought for a place of concealment. There were many available among the rocky little arroyos and gullies, but there was also no way to hide their horse tracks, should the trackers find them before Karin was able to travel again.

He left her with the horses and trotted toward the nearest little canyon, searched it futilely and went on. It took two hours to find what he was looking for and even then he had to settle for a hideout that wasn't too good. It was the cave of some large animal that had been long deserted and was dug out beneath a huge tree under a little cutbank. But it was large enough anyway, so he went back, gathered her into his arms and trotted to the dry little cave with its musty smell. Here he made up a pallet of moss and dry grass and laid her upon it. As he did so the beaded robe slipped a little at the shoulder, and he caught a glimpse of the skin there. It was raised in an angry weal. Drawing in his breath in consternation, he knelt beside her; lifted away the mass of dark hair at the nape of her neck, pulled aside the sleeve of the ceremonial dress. And he swore at what he saw.

The girl was a mass of bruises.

The sensation of fury was overpowering. He had to dig his nails into his own palms to overcome it. Karin had been travelling on fortitude, of which small store had been left to her after Plume and his Sits-Beside-Him-Woman had done with her. She had been starved, she had been beaten, slave-driven.

And he—poor fool—had thought she could travel alongside him as old Jules would have done. The rocking gait of the Indian horses must have been unbelievable torture to her aching frame; the long, cold journey, unbearable strain on a physique already tried to its limit.

Well, now he must admit the truth. Karin was too ill and too weak to go any further in her present condition. At the relentless pace needed to keep ahead of the Bloods, he would be leading her straight to her death. An hour or two's rest was no use to her; she needed days.

It was over an hour before she opened her eyes, gazed at him out of a flushed face, and blinked drowsily. He smiled, but it was a poor example of a smile at best.

"Karin, why didn't you tell me things were so bad with you?"

"We couldn't have stopped," she said truthfully.

"No," he answered slowly, "but we could have forted up maybe."

"Where are we?"

"In an old cave. Now listen to me. I'm going to cover you up and leave you here. I'll cover the entrance to the cave too. You stay here and don't make a sound. They'll track us here, maybe. I've got an idea that may draw 'em off. But no matter what happens, don't you make a sound. Just lie here an' rest so's you'll be strong when I get back."

She didn't say anything, but the mounting terror in her glance was more apparent than anything she could have said anyway. He frowned a little, reached down and caught her feverish hand and held it tightly.

"You're as safe as I can make you, Karin. Just remember—don't make a sound."

"How long will it be?"

He knocked out his pipe without looking at her. "I don't know. Until I can find some white men or some friendlies. It won't be any longer'n I can help, though." He glanced over at her. She looked even more appealing with her high, feverish colour and unblinking stare.

He bent very swiftly and kissed her fully on the mouth.

"Good-bye, ma'm. I'll be back, believe in that." Then he went out and made a clever job of camouflaging the maw of the cave. He hurried over to the rested horses, swung up and herded them south after making a lot of concealing tracks that covered his moccasin marks.

The sunlight was dazzling. It shone with rare brilliance off the steaming earth and made his back muscles relax for the first time in days. It also made the exhaustion within him clamour for attention. He had trouble making him mind concentrate. The tendency was for it to wander. Irritably, he correctly attributed this to the terrible punishment he'd handed himself for several days. But the new peril and its attendant anxiety kept him alert.

He rode south until he came to a sloping landswell, and there he herded the horses atop it and sat looking back over the country they had travelled. An hour later he slid off his horse and began to search for dried twigs. These he found after considerable effort and made into a little tipi-shaped cooking-fire, but he didn't strike fire to the thing for another two hours, and by then the sun was high overhead.

The waiting was the hardest. He thought back to the tracks and knew any hunter with the time would be able, after a bit, to unravel the mystery of the confusing horse tracks. He was planning a bold move to offset that possibility.

In the early afternoon he saw them coming. A lean line

116

of tawny horsemen with the winter sun flashing off their musket barrels and lance tips. He grunted to himself, looked at his horses, found them drowsing hip-shot in the warmth, and for the first time, he grinned. It was a savage, bitter smile, but it was full of defiance too.

The Blackfeet came slowly. They only made good time when the tracks they were obviously following led out in a direct route. Seth counted them. Seven. There would be others after Jules and Doctor Baird, but he shook off those thoughts. These seven would be brave and wily warriors. The pick of the soldier societies.

He hunkered by the little fire and struck his flint and steel. It was slow to start because the punky wood retained the earlier atmospheric dampness. Seth cursed and worried at it until some of the dry moss caught. He stayed only seconds longer, to make sure the licking fingerling of flame was going to live, then he went to the horses, mounted the big, rawboned Crow warhorse, growled at the others and drove them in a belly-down run.

He crossed a narrow valley and continued due south on the far side of it, hugging the west wall in order to have ready access to a hiding-place, should it become necessary to cache. An hour later he reined up and looked back. The little wisp of smoke from a cooking-fire was rising straight up into the burnished splendour of the sunny daylight. He smiled crookedly, herded his horses down to where a little glade offered scant pickings for them, then rode up a slope on his right and sliding to the ground, squatted beside his winded horse, watching.

He was no more than four miles from the finger of smoke and he dared go no farther for fear he wouldn't be able to see the Siksika bucks when they dashed up the hill. The worry was great though, that they might not hasten forward and so ignore the tracks he'd made around Karin's hideout.

Movement off to his right brought him upright gripping his rifle. It couldn't be the Bloods and it had been too vague and wispy to be buffalo. Swiftly, he led his horse down off the ridge, hobbled it and crept back to lie belly-down, watching with his heart in his mouth. A crisis was impending. He could feel it and the weariness dropped away like a blanket.

Then he saw them and understood. Four stealthy shapes making their way towards the ruse of a cooking-fire he'd built. Four warriors afoot. The Crows! He bit his lower lip and watched. They were stalking the fire, fanned out and deadly. In an instant Seth was on his feet running for his horse. He mounted it on the fly and fled back down to where he'd left the other animals, rounded them up and drove them east over a little series of erosion gullies and hills. There he swung them north and rode in among them reaching out with his rifle to whack them unmercifully on the ribs and rumps. Startled, the animals leapt away from him, went racing blindly and frenziedly back up the way they had come. Toward the hill where the fire burned.

Certain the animals wouldn't slacken pace for a while, Seth reined up and blew his own animal; sat there and watched the course of the Crow horses with his two Blood animals among them, and breathed excitedly. An ironic twist of fate had offered him an opportunity he hadn't been long in making the most of.

The Crow warriors, discovering the loss of their horses, had struck out like rabid wolves—which they were anyway—hunting for sign of the animals or the man who had taken them. By driving the beasts upland, back toward where the cooking-fire burned, he was sure the Crows would see them and converge on the spot where they would slow down to graze. The little slope where the fire was!

When his animal was fresh enough again, Seth turned and went back across the hills to the tight valley where he had been, and there he hobbled the horse and scurried back up to the eminence to watch.

The Crows had seen their horses and were running east, across the tumbled terrain to head them off. They were employing caution in a sense, but more important to them, and with good reason, was the re-acquisition of their riding animals.

Seth swung his head and watched the Bloods loping toward the hill too. He was crawling with excitement, for the Blackfeet had spurned the tracks and were heading right past the place where Karin lay. He thought that she must be able to hear the drumroll thunder of their galloping horses. Then, unexpectedly, one of the Bloods must have scented an ambush ahead. He reined up in a stiff-legged slide and held his lance aloft. The other Indians slowed and bunched up around him. At that moment the Crows burst into view streaming out onto the flat ground trying to effect a surround of their horses. Evidently, in their eagerness and exultation, they had neglected to look northward. The Bloods were sitting there, watching them.

Seth jumped up, hurried down to his horse and rode back very slowly. There would be a savage fight now. He was still a long way off when he heard an unfamiliar cry and surmised the Crows had seen their traditional enemies. Spurring up the closest hill he saw the Bloods make their initial charge. Two of the Crows were mounted, the other two had turned to face the unexpected attack, forgetting the horses in their astonishment. Both sides, however, were out for blood.

Seth ignored his exposed position and watched. The Bloods raised the yell. It drifted faintly to him. They were riding in a loosely held line, charging fiercely at the unprepared Crows. But the enemy Indians were strong-hearts too. Except to draw a little closer to one another, they didn't give any ground, so that when the Bloods swept within bow-range, they let off their first arrows and made the silence crumble with terrible Crow war shouts.

Seth rode over the side of the hill then, and reined up so that his horse was hidden but he, astride it, still had an uninterrupted view of the savage little battle.

The Bloods had smashed through the Crows, but now there were two riderless horses trailing them and one Crow was sprawled in the flat indifference of death. The Bloods raced out of range and re-grouped while the two mounted Crows used that moment to catch horses and drag them toward the unmounted man. He grabbed at the nearest animal and flung himself aboard. What the Crows did then, surprised Seth.

They raised their voices in off-key war-chants and charged straight into the Bloods. Three Crows to five Bloods. For some reason the Bloods were unnerved by the audacity or swiftness of the charge. They hesitated for a moment, then broke. Two raced eastward, out around the Crows, and three more went westward.

Seth understood the strategy if the Crows didn't. He was watching grimly when the Blackfeet all dropped over the far sides of their horses and loosed a volley of war-arrows from under the animals' necks. The Crows had understood the manœuvre at the last minute and had tried to rein around so as to face their enemies, thus presenting less of a target. It didn't work for two of them. Although no Crows were struck, two of them were unhorsed when their mounts crumbled under them, arrow shafts sticking out of their sides, just behind the shoulder.

Then the Bloods whooped triumphantly and swung in to close with the besieged outlanders. Seth longed to crawl close enough to pick off a Blood or two, but didn't do it. Not that he felt any urge to help the Crows, who were just as murderous as the Bloods, but because he had recognised the foremost Blackfoot warrior as Plume.

He didn't wait after that, but struck southward again in a long-legged slow lope. It carried him along the ridge for every Indian to see before he dipped finally, twisting backwards toward the fighting men, and went down the west side of the hill, back to the narrow valley below.

He knew the fight would be over in another half an hour or less. He knew also, that some of the Indians must have seen him. After that he rode steadily, sure they would follow him. Sure also that at least the Bloods would know who he was.

The unexpected stroke of good fortune that had put him in a position to steer the Crows against their ancient enemies had also provided Karin with more protection than Seth had hoped for. But, except for his quick grasp and wily planning, chances were that the Crows would have seen the seven Bloods and avoided them.

He kept south until he came to a spit of snow-water that was widening an already formidable erosion gully, and there he sought out a high point, rode up it and blew his horse while looking back.

The battle was over. He knew that despite the fact that he couldn't see the battlefield. The proof was in the fact that two Bloods were following his tracks along the ridge at a trot. One of them he knew by sight. The distance was vast, but not so vast as to obscure the gaudy lance with its unmistakable scalplocks. Plume held it vertically as he rode, head down and dark face twisted into new ugliness as he scented the end of the trail that he rode.

Seth watched a long time. Until at last, five Bloods were coming over his backtrail, then he smiled bitterly. There had been seven. The Crows had accounted for two at the cost of their own four lives. He turned his horse once more and rode down into the gently curving valley that would lead him straight south to Three Forks, and from now on it would be a race. Not a race of speed but a race of endurance. The Bloods and the white man both knew that their horses were wearying.

Wiles, not speed, would determine who was to be the victor, who the vanquished, in the ruthless contest they were joined in now. Seth rode with one eye on his Crow warhorse and the other on the terrain. If there was a way to favour the big, rawboned beast, he used it.

The landfall he was riding over sloped gently southward, as though it had expedited the course of some long-extinct river's march down the land to the sea. There were occasional patches of new grass, without strength of course, but still better than nothing to his famished horse. He dared to make several stops long enough for the animal to graze while he scrambled to some little hilltop and looked back at the pursuit.

The five Bloods were still coming. They were distant and moving slowly, inexorably, but they were like wolves on his trail. He smiled icily back at them. If they caught him, at least they wouldn't get Karin. Whether he made it to Three Forks and found some of the wintering mountain men there or not, the girl had plenty of pemmican to last her until Jules would find her.

He went back, sprang upon the Crow horse's back and heeled him out again, still wearing the unpleasant little smile. It was all the less prepossessing in view of the filthiness of his face, with its beard stubble and grey-weariness. Riding steadily, he thought of Jules with a sense of inner warmth. The old trapper would find the girl regardless of whether Seth came in alive or not. He was that kind.

The daylight waned early. Twilight was stalking the wilderness one moment. The next it had cast out a great purple blanket and obscured everything. Winter nights in the northern Indian country come like that.

The ghost of a man, slumped and bone-weary, with blood-shot eyes, half feverish, half irrational, rode down the night on the big, unkempt-looking Crow horse with an eagle feather dangling from its foretop. A spectre rider and a grisly ghost of a war-horse.

CHAPTER SEVEN

THE worst of the chase now began, for Seth was reeling with exhaustion. He sought about for a reserve of energy. There was none. Once he threw up his head at the sense of alarm that came drunkenly to warn him, and found that he was slumped over on his horse while the animal was grazing along with no thought to the stupefied burden on its back.

After that he rode as far as the next plum thicket along a creek, got down and foraged for wild grapevines out of which he made several lengths of primitive rope and lashed himself to the animal's back. The possibility of the Bloods staying on his trail after dark was remote for the elemental reason that, should they go astray in the darkness, they would lose much time picking up his tracks come dawn. Despite this, he kept going.

Several times later he awakened to find the horse pushing through willows in search of more feed. The whipping branches stung him back to life. Each time he reined the beast around and forced him in the general direction of Three Forks.

He never knew how much actual sleep he got that night, for he seemed to travel in a sort of silent vacuum of gloom that was liberally laced with bitter cold. Along toward dawn, the weather warmed perceptibly, and as he looked up at the sky through eyelids that felt as though there were fine grains of sand under them, he thought of how old Jules would sniff every time the weather changed. That forced his mind to the present and he conjectured on Jules's course and how much luck he'd had escaping. Doctor Baird entered his thoughts only as a wispy recollection without importance.

Full daylight was slow coming, for a leadenness was in the overcast again. There was the familiar metallic smell too, that meant snow. He sought sluggishly for a little rise and rode up the first one he saw, slid off his horse and sat down, waiting.

The chill left gradually but the daylight wasn't much better as far as visibility was concerned. Still, he sat there and smoked for breakfast and spat often—and watched. There was no sign of the Bloods. He was tempted to stretch out and close his eyes, but cursed instead and forced himself upright. In that position he held to his vigil until the pipe went out, then he mounted with difficulty and struck overland again.

Gradually now, the country took on a familiarity. It made him exult with a sardonic grimness. Three Forks wasn't far ahead. Another half day's ride. Then his mind suggested the possibility that the trappers and friendlies might not be there. It was still a long time until spring, but they might have left anyway. Be making their way leisurely down through Shoshoni country toward Pierre's Hole.

He shook his head and laughed so that the horse flicked his ears backwards. If there was no help at Three Forks, at the mountain men's hidden wintering site, then there would be no help at all. Seth knew that the Crow horse would never stand the longer trip to Pierre's Hole no matter how he was favoured.

The will to survive was all that kept him going. That, and the nagging worry about Karin, back there in the heart of hostile Indian country warm and hidden, but unable to defend herself.

More dead than alive he made the last five miles into the Three Forks congestion of mountains that broke out across a little valley to where two large creeks ran through. The Crow horse was still travelling well; no stumbling or

124

head-down lassitude, when they were pinched in among the hillocks and forced to take one of the broad game and Indian trails that led to the valley beyond.

Seth's blood-shot eyes roved constantly. He took heart from a wisp of smoke that braced the dreary atmosphere but made no more effort to hurry. It wouldn't matter now whether he loped into the wintering spot or not. If they were there, Jules and Bill Williams and the others, he'd find them shortly. If not—it wouldn't make any difference whether he hurried or not.

He reined up finally and lifted his head. The smell of smoke was stronger. It had a wonderfully revitalising effect on him. He slid down and led his horse, walking to stir life back into torpid, nearly numb limbs. Was still walking, in fact, when two Indian hunters ahead on the trail turned and looked back in astonishment as he called out to them.

"How-la."

The older of the two was carrying a freshly killed buck deer. The blood from the animal still steamed. He turned and stared, then grunted at Seth. They waited until the white man came up before either spoke. Then it was the stalwart, older buck. "You come alone?"

Seth nodded his head slightly. "Yeh. From the Blackfoot country. There are five Bloods trailing me. Warriors."

The buck stared and his mouth flattened a little. "How long back?"

"Maybe half a day; maybe more." He spoke again, as the three of them turned to walk along the trail toward the winter camp. "Beaver Killer here?"

"No. No Beaver Killer. He-Travels-Alone is. Others too."

He-Travels-Alone. Bill Williams. Seth felt warm thinking of the irascible, whining old trapper whose independence was a legend in the mountains. He wondered about Jules and decided that he and Baird hadn't made as good time as Seth had. He'd wait out the day. Maybe even wait overnight too. Then, if Jules didn't come in, he'd go back and look for him. He was going to need Jules to help him bring Karin in, past those hunting Bloods.

None of them spoke again until they were in among the lodges and colourful little soddies—log and mud houses that were half underground, half above. No settlement had ever looked so good to Seth. He was turning to lead his horse toward a gaudily decorated lodge with at least twenty-eight lodge-poles sticking up above the weather-flap, which he knew from pictographs would house old Bill Williams, when the big Shoshoni warrior reached over and touched his arm.

"No many more Bloods?"

"No. Just those five. There were seven. Crows killed two."

The buck grunted again and cast a long glance at Seth's Crow horse. "You kill Crows?"

"No. I stole their horses. They fought the Bloods. All Crows killed. Four of them. Two Bloods."

"They come how?"

"Over my tracks." Seth got the drift of the man's thoughts and shook his head. "You wait. I'll get Bill and the others. We'll all go back. I hid a girl back there. You wait."

"No wait," the Shoshoni said gruffly. "They might come heap fast.

Seth shook his head quickly. "No. They can't come here. Not enough of them. You wait."

The buck looked at Seth's battered, grey features, then turned abruptly and headed off among the skin tipis scattered around through the trees and brush above the valley. Seth watched him go with his younger companion following like a worshipful little dog; then he continued on around the trail to Bill Williams's lodge, hobbled the Crow horse and went inside.

Old Bill's gargoyle features lifted when Seth entered. He was squatting drowsily before the fire-hole on a fabulously thick hair-on buffalo robe. He blinked once. That was the only indication he made of his staggering surprise. Then he grunted.

"God a'mighty, boy, you look like a ghost. Here, set down here." Bill turned and spoke haltingly to a buxom squaw with a perfectly round, moon-like face, and sturdy body to match. "Fetch us some gruel, Star. The boy's plumb drawed out."

Seth sat and ate. Bill plied him with questions until Seth had related the entire story, then old Bill swore in a sing-song way. Unwinding his great stringy length, he went over to the tent-flap and poked his head, yelling something in Shoshoni. A young buck came up and listened to Bill for a moment, then turned without a word and headed over toward the lodge where a grim looking warrior was gutting an animal that hung suspended from a tree limb. Bill went back around Seth and dropped down on the big robe again, studying his face.

"You ain't seed Jules since you run for it?"

"No."

"You sure you could find whar you cached the female again?"

"Certain, Bill." Seth belched, wiped at his mouth and ran one hand through the thick nap of the buffalo robe on his side of the fire. "I'm tuckered, Bill. Let me catch a few hours' sleep, then we'll go back and hunt up Jules —and get the girl. All right?"

Bill didn't answer. He didn't have to, for Seth lay back in the permeating warmth of the tipi, rolled over to shade his eyes from the flickering light of the cooking-fire, and in a second was sound asleep.

Bill sat there and smoked his pipe, thinking. After a while he knocked out the dottle, got up and stalked out of the lodge. Seth didn't hear it but Bill's woman did; he was talking to himself as he always did, only now the whining tones were softer, more garrulous and unpleasant sounding.

127

Seth wouldn't have awakened when he did, except for the bony claw shaking him by the shoulder. He opened swollen eyes and looked up into the villainous face of Old Bill. The firelight danced with bronze-red macabreness off the older man's features. He blinked and stretched. It was a luxurious movement and brought back a lot of little aches he'd forgotten for the moment.

"Up, boy, there's work to do."

"Like what?"

"I sent out scouts. Them Bloods're comin' close. You want to be in at their scalpin' or not? Don't make no difference to me. You kin go on a-sleepin' if you want, only I figured you'd want to see 'em danglin' a little."

Seth's instinctive desire was to stay exactly where he was forever. He got up, but stiffly, and groped around for his long-rifle. Bill mumbled something and handed him the weapon, stood aside and watched him stretch, then bob up and down several times on his sore legs.

"You've done a heap of movin', Seth," he said appraisingly. "An' you look it too."

"What did you expect, you old goat—a ceremonial get-up?"

Bill smiled and wagged his head. "Hear me, boy; them's varmints out there that you owe a killin' to, but if you don't feel able, Ol' Bill'll be glad to fetch you back their topknots."

Seth turned grimly toward the door-flap and passed out into the night. He was surprised and turned toward Bill Williams. "I didn't know I'd slept so long, Bill."

"Don't make no difference. Nothin' we could do 'till the skunks got close enough. There—that black horse—you can ride him. He's strong an' that wolf-bait you rode in ain't fit to do no chasin' or fightin' Injuns on. Let's go."

Seth mounted the black horse. The beast was surprisingly fat, for the middle of winter. Anyone less knowing would have marvelled. Not Seth; he knew the animal

128

had very recently been stolen from immigrants or settlers somewhere. They were the only people who had fat horses in the wintertime.

Bill Williams looked more grotesque than ever, astride his vicious-eyed little Indian horse. The beast's mane hadn't been curried in years, if ever. He was too small for Bill's fantastically long legs, and his sullen-defiant expression indicated a formidable disposition. But Bill sat up there, his great long legs tucked up and his body hunched forward, squinting at the conglomeration of Indians, whites and half-bloods that came riding up out of the night. He twisted his head and peered at Seth. "You lead us, boy. You just come over the trail an' know which way your tracks lay. Hear me, now; watch out for ambushes. Them scoundrels are mighty fine at that sort of work."

Seth eased around the others, saw their interested, inquisitive looks, and canted his rifle crossways over the little pad-saddle with bone stirrups he was riding. The thing was a blessing after the bony, relentless back of the rawboned Crow horse.

He had to go slowly because the sickle moon hadn't come up yet and the trail was a dark blur underfoot. Feeling his way, he wondered how many were in his war-party. The glimpse he'd had back by Bill Williams's tipi, hadn't been sufficient to more than make out silhouettes of men a-horseback. He shrugged to himself. It wouldn't make much difference. Even if the Bloods had rested—as he knew they must have, to be so far behind him—they still wouldn't be any match for the battlers in his wake.

The trail down from the funnel of Three Forks canyon was familiar enough. Where it dropped still more and debouched into the long, crooked valley he'd followed coming in, there were moist, opalescent cuttings of moonlight to light their way. The night had turned bitterly cold and the smell of snow was more pronounced than ever.

Seth halted when they were off the trail and in the valley. He turned and glanced over at Bill Williams. "Where're the scouts that you sent out?"

For answer Williams beckoned up a lean, very dark Shoshoni buck. The man looked inquiringly at Bill and listened to the flood of nasal, sing-song, grunting words, answered briefly and looked away from the white man, pointing. Bill interpreted for Seth. "He says they're up ahead about four, five miles yet."

"Well," Seth said irritably, "have him go ahead and show us."

Bill shrugged and relayed the instructions to the scout, who promptly reined around in front of Seth and struck off. The sound of horse's hooves on the ground got gradually louder and Seth knew the layer of frost on the ground was thickening. He felt remarkably refreshed and, except for the unnatural puffiness of his eyes and random aches in his legs, was feeling a lot better than he had when he'd first fled the Blackfoot village.

The men strung out in a loose line that effectively barred any egress past them down the valley. They rode that way for a long hour or so before the Shoshoni scout threw up his arm and slid off his horse. Seth saw nothing and smelled nothing, but he instantly followed suit as did all the others of his party. Two Indians were delegated the chore of guarding their horses and the other men clustered up around Seth and Bill Williams. The old mountain man puckered up his face and spat against the frozen earth, then turned and looked expectantly at Seth.

"You lead us, boy. These here are your Injuns. Mind you don't lead us into no ambush though."

Seth squatted and skylined the hills around them, saw nothing and straightened up with a frown. "Where are they?"

Bill asked the scout, who pointed on up the little valley and made a short, cutting motion with his arm.

130

Bill grunted. "Straight ahead. 'Bout a mile or such a matter, he says."

Seth looked at the men. There were at least twelve of them. Every one had a musket. For a moment that surprised him, then he recalled how Old Gabe had taken great pains to arm his Snake Indians—Shoshonis—and keep them supplied with shot and powder. He turned back and led out, motioning for the men to fan out in their former positions; covering the width of the valley so that when they came within firing range, each man would be an effective musketeer.

The cold was intensified when they stalked forward. It seemed to stream over the protecting little hills, the farther up the valley they went. Seth moved slowly, sniffing. It was an hour before he caught the scent, and then it wasn't a cooking-fire, but the strong odour of sweating horses. He wrinkled his nose and looked at his men. They were all glancing at one another, even Bill Williams. The smell of Blood horses was strong in the clear night air.

Seth knew that no Plains Indian ever fought at night. He also knew why. Warriors killed in the darkness were forever condemned to walk in the groping world of darkness unable to find their way into the Sand Hills. He smiled to himself. Of the other Blackfeet he had nothing more than a passive dislike, but for one—Plume—he had a fierce and eager feeling of personal hatred. He stopped when the smell of the horses was strongest and beckoned to Bill Williams, squatted and waited for the trapper to amble over. Bill dropped down, as did all the other stalkers.

"What have you got in mind, boy?"

"Send back a runner for our horses, Bill. Have them brought up where we can get on them in a hurry. Detach three of your best men to scout up their horses and stampede them. The rest of us'll wait here until we hear the horses being run off, then we'll charge 'em. All right?"

131

Bill nodded his head with a ghoulish smile. "You're a regular soldier, Seth. Hear me now, though—they'll scatter like quail if we give 'em half a chance. Runnin' off their critters'll warn 'em."

Seth shrugged. "They won't get far afoot. Your Snakes'd rather track 'em down in the daylight."

"Yeh," Bill agreed. "I allow." He got up stiffly and glanced up the dark little valley with its spilled-over moonbeams that lay jagged and uneven across the quickening frost on the ground. "All right, Seth. I'll give you the sign." He strode back to the hunkering, irregular line of 'breeds, whites and Shoshoni fighting men. Seth rubbed his arms and worked his toes inside his moccasins to liven up the circulation, then he looked to his rifle and priming, stood up finally and stood hip-shot, awaiting Bill's signal.

When it came, Seth had already seen the three Shoshonis jogging silently, trailing their guns, around to the west of the waiting men. Another man was trotting back down the valley. Seth watched him go knowing he'd bring up their horses and the guards left behind. He nodded and signalled back to Bill Williams and moved forward in a crouched stoop, rifle held in both hands and his eyes glued to the slit of faint iridescence that lay between heaven and earth.

The longest, hardest part of the stalking lay ahead. Seth kept pace with the others but a savage eagerness drummed inside his head. It was still drumming when a louder sound of the same nature broke into the silence and somewhere, up ahead and to his right, over toward the little erosion gullies across the valley, a shrill, wavering scream split the night. It made his hair stand up along the back of his head. He leapt erect and broke over into a lope, eastward.

By then the unmistakable sound of stampeded horses filled the darkness and the man who had made the shrill screech was being joined by others. But now the alarm was past and defiance was ringing in the war-cries of the Bloods. Seth threw back his head and gave a wild howl. This was instantly taken up by his warriors who made the night terrible with the victory scream of the Snakes. Even old Bill Williams's quavering, reedy voice added to the tumult with a nerve-racking shriek.

Seth ran across in front of several Shoshonis. They howled at him and raced over toward the bedlam of the Blackfoot bivouac. A rifle blast lashed out toward the shouting Shoshonis like a reddish dagger of flame. It only added to the wildness of the charging men's excitement.

Seth, however, stopped in his tracks when he saw the muzzleblast. He knew what he wanted to know. The position of the Bloods. Very carefully he knelt and shouldered his rifle, waiting. The darkness was too dense however, and the Bloods, knowing their only escape lay in remaining motionless, used the natural camouflage wisely. They stopped their noise and flattened upon the ground.

Seth was still kneeling, waiting, when Bill Williams squirmed over beside him and grunted. "For only five of 'em, they're goin' to make a fight of it, boy."

"They're strong-hearts," Seth said, without looking around. "There's one there I want for myself."

"Ugh," Bill grunted. "Why'n't you challenge 'im?"

Seth lowered his rifle slowly. Off to his right were vague, wispy shadows that emerged out of the night and faded out just as quickly. His warriors from Three Forks. He turned the idea over in his head and knew he was in no physical shape for a knife or hatchet fight. But he stood up slowly and squinted toward the area where the besieged Blackfeet were. There was another way, and after all, he had no grudge agains the other Bloods.

Leaning on his rifle, he jutted his head a little and waited for a lull in the racket the besiegers were making, to shout out in Siksika.

"You Bloods. You will die. Your horses are gone. You cannot get away." Before he could say more a Blackfoot called out and taunted him. He waited again before continuing. "Hear me. I offer you a way to live." The silence settled quickly after that. Even the men from the Three Forks settlement were listening.

"Send out Plume, your great warrior. I will fight him with my rifle. We will duel it out. If he lives, you can have your freedom but nothing else. If I live you must give your horses and weapons to the Snakes; but I will ransom your lives to the Snakes and you can walk back to Black Horse's band."

There was a long, drawn out silence while both sides digested Seth's challenge. Those who didn't understand Siksika hurried over to where Bill Williams was standing, a little apart from Seth, and plied him with questions. The only sound was Bill's whining voice making interpretations.

Seth waited, leaning on his rifle. He felt no especial anxiety, even though he knew that at close range the war-bow of the Blood warrior was a far more deadly weapon than his single-shot rifle.

As in the case of Black Horse's answer about aiding them escape, Plume's acceptance of the challenge was done in an oblique fashion. He didn't answer the white man. Instead, out of the darkness came the war-song of a mighty Blood warrior. Seth and Bill Williams knew, as did the vastly intrigued 'breeds and Snake Indians, that Seth's challenge had been accepted by a strong-heart among the stalwart Blackfeet.

Seth was still leaning on his rifle, waiting for the victory song to end, when Bill Williams ambled up and stooped, squinting from bright little weasel-eyes, at Seth.

"I can drop him afore he gets to you, Seth. Just say the word an' I'll pluck off his hair like a squirrel's head." Bill's inquisitive glance was shiny and unblinking.

Seth shook his head. "No," he said slowly, "I've got

reasons for wanting to kill this one myself, Bill. But there's a favour you *can* do for me."

"Call it, boy. Ol' Bill's a pardner t'any friend o' ol' Jules."

"What I said about the other Bloods. About letting them go back. I've got bales of skins at Jules's and my cache—you saw them—"

"Yep. I seed 'em. Couple of thousand dollars' worth, boy." But Old Bill looked extremely pained. "Now listen, Seth," he whined protestingly. "You're not figurin' to parcel 'em out to these Snakes an' 'breeds for the hides of them mangy Bloods, be you?"

"Yeh. That's exactly what I want you to promise me, Bill. That you'll buy those Blackfeet off from the Snakes and 'breeds an' white trappers from Three Forks. Let 'em go back to Black Horse's band at Moon Prairie."

"Aw," Bill whined, disgusted and anguished both, by the payment of such a sum for four or five enemy Indian bucks. "Seth, you've lost your reason, boy. Ain't no Injun on earth worth that much, an' that's a fact. Hear me now, boy—I can talk 'em out of botherin' them danged Blackfeet without havin' to pay 'em a copper. You jest leave it to ol'—"

"No thanks, Bill," Seth said dryly. "I want it done my way and I want you to give me your word you'll do it like that."

Bill writhed in his tracks, evidently fighting a valiant inward battle with his scruples—or lack of scruples. An entire season's catch for less than half a dozen danged Blackfeet. He almost moaned at the thought. Seth turned and flashed him a long, hard look.

"Bill, I know you danged well. If you steal my pelts and keep them I'll come back an' haunt the hell out of you. You an' Jules both, just to keep you honest."

"Awright," Bill whined. "Awright, Seth—but you're an idiot, boy; but awright; I'll pass you my word on it."

They stood with altogether different expressions, listening to the haranguing song of Plume, who was reciting his greatest coups and extolling his prowess as a great fighting man. To Bill Williams, Indians, friendlies and hostiles alike, were nothing more than animals. He tolerated them, lived among them, fought them, killed them and robbed them, as well as made friends with them, all with the same off-hand indifference. In time his lifelong policy of piracy would get him killed, but that was a long way off yet. Right then he stood, stooped, squint-eyed and sour-looking, peering toward the sound of the Blackfoot's war-song, and his face reflected only great scorn and complete disgust. One for the Blood warrior, the other for the waiting white man who was beside him, leaning patiently on his long-rifle waiting for Plume to stop his war-chant.

The vibrating, strong voice died out finally, and into the long silence came the man's call out of the darkness. "Are you the white man called Medicine-Walker?"

"I am," Seth answered.

Plume made a savage grunt that they all heard. The Three Forks men were hunkering in little groups, enthralled. "How do we know your tongue is straight?"

"What proof do you want?" Seth called back.

That seemed to stump the Blackfeet. Actually—and everyone knew it—there was nothing they could depend upon under the circumstances but Seth's word. They were surrounded and afoot. They were quite helpless. Plume showed his perplexity when he spoke out again.

"We want to hear the men of your war-party say we can go back alive after I kill you."

Seth turned and nodded at Bill Williams. Despite the look of contempt and anger that shone from the old trapper's ugly face, he called out to his men. They listened to him, then shouted back their promise to do as Seth wished. Bill relayed this to Seth, who in turn translated it into Blackfoot and called it out to Plume. Another long silence ensued. Seth made no motion to hurry the

Blackfeet. There was no reason to hurry anyway. They were all shivering and as cold as they could be.

"We can keep our horses to ride back on?"

Seth cursed in English. "No. Whether you kill me or I kill you, your horses, your weapons—anything you have that the Snakes want—will be taken from you. You will be alive—some of you—and that is all."

Apparently Plume heard the impatience and irritation in Seth's voice, for he took no more time to counsel with his companions. "All right," he called back. "How is it we will fight?"

Seth straightened up off his rifle barrel and lifted the gun up, reaching down automatically to brush off the butt-plate before he swung it horizontally across his waist. He held it lightly with both hands.

"It is simple. You will tell your warriors to stay where they are. I will tell my men to do the same thing. You and I will then walk toward each other. It is dark. There is much ground to be covered. When we are close enough to see, we will try to kill one another. Is that understood?"

Plume answered even as Bill Williams's indignant, profane and reedy voice muttered an undertone. The Blackfoot's answer was the more easily understood because it was louder. "It is agreed. When will we start?"

Seth turned aside annoyedly and glanced up at Bill. "What'd you say?"

"Oh, you fool, you, Seth, you got one shot. He's got a fist full of arrows. You miss or not an' he'll make a porcupine out of you. Let me tell you how to do it. I been in—"

"No. I want it this way." Seth turned back toward the Blackfeet. "When you are ready, yell!"

The tension mounted as the seconds went by.

Seth raised his rifle, looking carefully to its priming. He ran a hand damp in the palm down over the smooth old hickory stock, and stood wide-legged with the gun held ready in both hands.

137

He looked over at the Three Forks men. The wintering whites were indistinguishable from the 'breeds and full-bloods. They were all squatting like graven images, watching and waiting; now and then a grunt or a ripple of speech would run among them. Mostly they were as silent as the dark spot where the beseiged Bloods were.

Bill Williams drew off a little and turned his head for a long look at Seth's motionless silhouette, then he squatted too, and brought his rifle up close so that he could see the hammer and run his grimy thumb over it. He cocked the piece very carefully so as to make no noise, then fingered out several newly moulded rifle balls and popped them into his mouth. After that he reached down and tugged his powderhorn around so that it hung athwart his chest for easy access. Old Bill was ready.

A thoroughly experienced mountain man could reload his long-rifle with surprising speed, but his best time could be easily beaten by a seasoned Indian bowman. The disparity in armament was especially noticeable—and lethal —at close quarters. The range of the two weapons was about the same. Smooth-bore rifle and powerful war-bow both were deadly for quite a distance, but no mountain man ever fired his single-shot gun until he had to. In fact, no two mountain men ever fired simultaneously. Instinct had prompted Old Bill to get set to fire the second shot; that and his ingrained idea that no white man should ever give an Injun an even break if he could help it.

Seth mouthed two more rifle balls even though he knew he wouldn't get a chance to reload if he missed the first time. Nervously, he tugged his powderhorn up a little, too, and that was another wasted motion. He knew it when he did it. But a man who has never let his gun get out of reach, has literally slept with it to keep the working parts from becoming dampened or frozen or rusted, had certain purely automatic reflexes. These Seth indulged in now, while he waited for the ear-splitting cry Plume would give before he bounded forward out of the night. Plume would have one arrow nocked into his bow and at least one more between two fingers of his left hand while a third would be more than likely held lightly between his teeth.

The Blackfeet were deliberately drawing out the minutes. Seth and Bill Williams and the other white men knew it. The Indians knew it too, but they didn't understand it so much for what it was—an unnerving process. It was simply that they appreciated the spine-tingling tension it made.

Then Plume roared out his war-cry. The scream shattered the black stillness into a hundred fragments that were little echoes chasing one another out through the gloom.

Seth dropped to one knee without advancing a step. He waited until he was sure the Blood warrior must be stalking him, then very deliberately he reached up under the barrel of his rifle and withdrew the wiping-stick. It was an oaken ramrod and worn smooth from much use. He propped the thing against his leg and held his gun up a little so that the maw of the thing was slanting enough to bear upon a standing man.

That was his first mistake.

The stillness grew until it was literally a syrup of stickiness in the little valley. Seth felt sweat running along the furrows under his shaggy beard. Somewhere, out there ahead of him, was the only man on earth he'd ever wanted to kill badly enough to risk his own life without thought of consequences.

But Plume didn't come rushing in as Seth thought surely he would. There wasn't a sound in the ground nor a reverberation. Seth made a wry face. The Blood was stalking him then; using the night as his ally. Very slowly Seth went down flat and swung his powderhorn off his chest so that it was lying beside his right elbow, alongside the ramrod,

More waiting. More silence. More gut-constricting tension and more vivid understanding that soon a tufted, stubby little arrow would come out of the blackness, searching for his flesh with its barbed, rusty tip.

Skylining helped Seth see. By not looking directly ahead, but by seeing with the outer extremities of his eyes —the oldest of all Indian tricks—he was able to probe a little farther around him for sign of movement. But when he finally saw it, there was no attempt on Plume's part to conceal the quick, vicious, blurring movement of his glistening arm where it had drawn back by his ear and let go the gut-string of his bow with a terrible whistling sound.

Seth rolled as soon as he saw the movement, came to rest on his belly again and jerked his gun up. The shadows were closing down again, with their obscurity and stillness, but he drew the faintly darker lump on the ground over his sights. Let it race back down the barrel to his eyes—and fired.

Several men shouted in spite of themselves. Bill Williams was swearing terribly. He was prone now too, but he dared not shoot despite a consuming eagerness to, for he couldn't see either Seth or the Blood Indian.

Seth went over on his side without waiting to guess whether he had killed Plume or not. With fingers sweat-greasy, he held the rifle barrel, poured in powder recklessly, spat in the ball and was ramming it with quick, frantic motions when he heard the triumphant shout of Plume.

The big Blood was on his feet. Seth knew that because he had felt the vibrations in the earth under him as Plume had leapt up. Sweat oozed out under his clothes.

With a tremendous shout, the Blackfoot jumped forward and glared about him. He repeated this motion three times, then he howled again and went charging forward with his bow tugged back and the arrow ready.

Seth could hear him coming. He knew that the slightest motion would be caught by the wild glare of his enemy. He lay perfectly still with his right hand still on the wiping-rod. Rolling over once, he came up to a sitting position and he was levelling the rifle when the Blood came charging out of the darkness. Seth didn't hesitate despite the fact that the ramrod was dangling ridiculously from the end of his gun. He fired as the warrior slammed to a halt and swung like a striking snake, bringing his bow to bear.

The second shot brought up a rousingly hopeful cheer from the Three Forks men and a blistering, uneven string of blasphemies from the high-pitched twang of frustrated, wildly excited Bill Williams.

Seth saw Plume's war-bow jump under the impact of the released gut-string but he had no time to move. What happened after that was too fast to take account of. A terrible tug at his head that swung him off balance, then a release just as sudden that left him lying on his side. He reached out frantically for his rifle and fought to get up. There was a rippling, sticky warmth running along his cheek and neck, down under the ragged collar of his hunting shirt.

He sprang up with his rifle swinging. Where Plume had been though, was nothing.

He stopped and looked down. The big Blood was lying there with his eyes wide open and his mouth working as though tugged by cords he had no control over. Seth dropped his rifle and drew out his hatchet. There was a roaring sound in the right side of his head as he stooped. It distracted him just enough. He never swung the toma-hawk, but stood balanced forward on his toes, staring into the Blackfoot's face.

Very slowly the seconds ticked off. He straightened up and raised his head, looked around where he knew the other Bloods would be, and, making his voice as calm as he could, called out to them.

"Plume is down. He is vanquished. Leave your bows

and lances and muskets. Walk out here with your hands out in front of you. Move slowly. Your lives depend on it."

He reached up and felt the side of his face and head. It was covered with blood, and yet there was no sense of pain. Wonderingly he explored with fingertips until he found the wound. The lobe of his right ear was completely gone. Plume's arrow had come that close.

He faced toward where Bill Williams's whine was calling out to him. "I got him, Bill. I told the other Blackfeet to come out unarmed. Tell the Three Forks men not to shoot at them but to bring their guns and walk over here where I am."

Bill's garrulous cursing came back. It stopped long enough for the trapper to interpret what Seth had said, then Bill began shambling into the darkness, eyes wolf-bright and searching.

CHAPTER EIGHT

PLUME was dying.

Worse than that though, was the way he was doing it. Seth's wiping-stick had splintered under the explosive impact of his second shot. Where the rifle ball went no one ever knew, but the split ramrod had gone as straight as any arrow. Had, in fact, pierced Plume all the way through so that when he fell backwards the sharpened, splintered ends were driven into the ground. He was skewered.

He lay there fully conscious, his mouth still working even after the defeated Bloods came forward slowly. They took a long look at their vanquished leader and broke out into soft, wailing death-chants.

Bill Williams shouldered past the Three Forks men, glanced once, contemptuously, at the dying Blackfoot, and ordered some of the Snakes to go fetch the Blackfoot weapons. He turned and regarded Seth with something very close to towering disgust, and spoke. His voice was even more whining and plaintive than usual.

"I seen fools, boy. Big uns an' little uns and red uns an' white uns—but of 'em all, you're the biggest." He flicked one claw-like hand toward the glazing eyes of Plume. "An' you'd do it for a skunk like that. 'Tain't sensical, I tell you. Jules'd agree with me. An' how'd you come to miss that first shot?"

Seth was reloading his rifle. When he finished he leaned on the weapon and looked up at Bill Williams. "My eyes didn't focus right, Bill. Too tired I reckon."

143

He glanced at the dying man, felt no pity and lifted his head to stare at the four remaining Blackfeet. He had seen every one of them around the dance-fire the morning he'd made his run for it. "You Bloods, walk ahead of us. There will be many guns on your backs. Run and you will die." He turned toward old Bill. "Send a couple of men along with 'em. Let's go back; I'm about done for."

Bill looked at the handsome scalplock of Plume. The braids were carefully ensconced in white weasel skins and there were gee-gaws worked into the rest of the thick matt. "You want his hair, boy?"

Seth turned away without answering. That was *one* facet of life on the farthest frontier he had never mastered, nor tried to master.

He jerked his head toward the horses the Three Forks men were holding, and walked away in silence. Bill stood where he was, watching Seth get to horse. He made no move to go even after the others were mounted and waiting.

Seth kneed out the black horse and made no attempt to guide the beast after it had found the wide trail that swung up along the west side of the narrowing heights. He made no attempt to hold off the thraldom either. It held him in a lassitude all the way back to Bill Williams's lodge, where he dismounted, turned the animal loose and went through the tipi-flap with the war-bridle and pad-saddle in one hand, his long-rifle in the other.

Bill's stocky squaw looked up inquiringly, smiled and pointed toward a black iron pot that was simmering on the fire. Seth ignored both the squaw and the pot. Threw down the bridle, dumped the pad-saddle on the thick buffalo robe, and lay down with his head on it. He didn't hear Bill or the others return. In fact he heard nothing at all until noon of the following day when a hand was shaking him roughly and he sat up with a swear word poised.

"Glad you made it, Seth."

He would never mistake that voice. He leapt up and grabbed at the worn-out looking man with both arms. "Jules!"

"'Tain't Black Horse, boy," Jules said in a hoarse, thick voice, "but b'gawd I nigh lost my hair to 'em at that. Give us a hell of a run for it afore we lost 'em."

Seth let Jules go and pointed toward the iron pot. The old trapper sat down stiffly with a fixed, fatigued smile on his face. Not until then did Seth notice Bill Williams across the fire, cross-legged and working diligently over a large willow circle that had a fleshed-out new scalp stretched within its perimeter. Bill was laboriously painting the skin side vermilion from a little stone pot he had beside him. Plume's scalp. Seth looked around and saw Jules's knowing glance. He shrugged.

"You bring Baird back, too?"

"Yeh," Jules said with a dry chuckle. "I couldn't have shook him off if I'd tried. Not after he seen them Bloods a-whoopin' it along after us."

"Did they follow you here, Jules?"

"Naw; I lost 'em about thirty, forty miles back. Come on to a regular hogback of stone. Left no tracks across that." Jules ate with both hands. The grease was thick over his chin in the mattress of his beard. "Whar's the girl?"

"I cached her. Had to, Jules. She was tuckered right out."

Jules made a clucking sound and looked over at Williams. "Bill, you scalp-lovin' ol' devil, why'n't you an' Seth go back an' fetch the female?"

"Ain't no hurry," Bill said laconically, holding his scalp loop out at arms length for them to admire.

Seth got up and put a hand on Jules's shoulder to hold him down when he started to rise. "You stay here,

Jules. Sleep, like I did. I'll go get her. I shouldn't have slept so long." He still looked exhausted, though.

Jules swore sulphurously at Bill Williams. His black eyes snapped despite their weariness. Old Bill put his scalp down reluctantly and made a screwed up face at Jules. "It's a-goin' ter snow," he said, as though that made rescuing Karin Baird unnecessary, some way.

Jules's profanity gathered venom and intensity until Bill got up with an ungracious curse of his own. "Awright, you old scoundrel," he whined. "I'll go with him, but I don't like it."

Seth was outside saddling Bill's stolen black horse when the gaunt trapper came out, sniffed, shuddered several times and went shamblingly after his own animal. He was carrying his rifle and two yearling buffalo robes. Seth waited for him to scramble aboard the ugly Snake horse he rode, then turned and struck out of Three Forks.

He had ridden for almost three hours into the early afternoon before he remembered the four surviving Blackfeet warriors. "Bill? What'd you do with the Bloods?"

"They're tied in a lodge. Don't fret, boy, ol' Bill's word's as good as—"

"Yeh. I know. That's why I asked."

Bill looked up with the same whining reproach in his face. "You're the most insultin' cuss I ever runned across, Seth, danged if you ain't."

They travelled all that afternoon and made a camp at dusk in a sheltered draw where there was new feed poking up among the willows. The smell of snow was stronger than it had been since Seth had first noticed it. Bill looked skyward often, and made a wheezing, sniffing sound.

"I don't like it, boy. Hear me now—she's a-goin' to bust loose and blizzard like hell. Mark me, boy."

Seth slept readily enough and at dawn was wide awake. There was a light skiff of snow on the hills and more falling. It wasn't anything more threatening than the usual

146

late winter downfall however. He had a tiny cooking-fire made and some pemmican warmed by the time Bill rolled out bleary-eyed and looked around.

"Could'a' swore," he said in a cracked voice, "we'd be buried under the stuff by sunup."

Seth smiled and jerked his head upwards. "There'll be more, Bill. Just be patient."

They rode all that day and by late afternoon the snow was forming up ahead of their horses. Seth was beginning to worry. He had the landmarks fixed well enough in his head, but he had ignored the thought he'd had before leaving Three Forks, about bringing an extra horse. Now it looked as if he should have.

Bill grunted and reined up at a likely camping spot but Seth shook his head at him. "On the way back, Bill. If we travel this slow for another day we might get snow-bound."

Bill looked aghast. Downright grieved. "You mean ride all night? Hear me, boy—she'll keep another day."

Seth didn't argue. He turned and kicked the black horse with his heels and rode off. Bill sat there dumb-founded and indignant, then he reined after the younger man with a steady monotone of profanity lining his wake.

The night grew stormy and bitterly cold. Seth had to get off and squat, skylining to get his bearings often. Bill shivered and whined an uninterrupted stream of cuss words.

Along before dawn Seth stopped altogether and got down with a helpless grunt. Old Bill peered down at him beneath craggy eyebrows that were ghostly white with frost. They added a striking emphasis to his hobgoblin features with the down-drooping nose and the upthrust chin.

"You lost, Seth? God a'mighty, a man could get lost awful easy a-beatin' around like this. We'd better just cache for a spell, I say."

"I'm not lost. We're here; only the damned snow's about blinded me. We'll wait until dawn."

They did, squatting with the buffalo robes around them, for all the world like Indians seeking medicine-visions. Unmoving, silent, humped over and huddled close together. They remained like that until a lighter hue came into the leaden sky, then Seth stood up, flexed his cramped legs and threw off the robe. He turned very slowly northward and squinted through the snowfall. Visibility was limited.

He started walking through the drifts with a puzzled frown.

Then he saw it. The huge, gaunt, supplicating old limbs of a large fir tree. Laden with snow and strangely beautiful in spite of its tortured posturings. The tree he had cached Karin under.

He moved faster. Was almost running, slogging, before he got close enough to make out the grass and sod covering he had built over her hideout.

Working with fingers stiff from cold and shaking in anxiety, Seth tore at the matting, calling Karin's name wildly, so that the wind that was coming up added to the fierceness of his cries.

When the dirt finally crumbled, he bent far over and peered into the burrow. Karin was looking up at him with a breathless mixture of terrible fright and wild relief. He ducked low and crawled over to her.

"Karin, I'm back. Lord—!"

"Oh, Seth." There was all the hoarded terror and gladness in the word and the name.

He reached out and she fell into his arms. He was sitting there rocking her back and forth when Bill poked his face into the opening, making snuffling sounds. He could feel her stiffening within his grasp and smiled down into the deeply violet light of her eyes. "That's Bill Williams. He came back with me."

148

"You made it? To Three Forks like you said you would try to?"

He nodded his head. "Yeh. I made it. So did Jules an' your pappy, Karin."

"Did the Indians find you?"

Bill was cracking his knuckles in the doorway, looking up squint-eyed at the sky. "The Injuns found him, lady, an' we done for 'em, but if you two'd sort of let go each other, we could make tracks out of here. This here's one buffalo don't want to get snowed under if he can help it."

Karin moved within the circle of Seth's arms. He didn't relinquish his grip until he remembered something he had to tell her, then he let her go with a hard smile. "And Karin—Plume's dead."

She was silent a moment, then turned her head slowly and looked up into his face. "I'm glad," she said fiercely. "I never thought I'd be glad when anyone was killed, but I am."

He picked up the half empty parfleche sack of pemmican and motioned Bill out of the doorway. They all crawled out and Seth helped her stand.

"Lord," he said uncertainly, "it's sure good to see you look—I mean—Karin, you like to scared me to death, the way you were when I left you."

She smiled up at him. "You must have thought me a fine sort of travelling companion. Seth, I'm sorry I gave way like that. I think if I'd had a good meal before I started out—and maybe two hours' sound sleep. . . . You don't blame me for it?"

"Blame you? Land sake, I was just glad to see you alive when I got back!"

"Oh, I soon caught up with a little of my old self. I reckon I slept solid the first day. And then I ate the food you left me." She found a deep chuckle from somewhere within her rounded throat. "But that pemmican, Seth—!"

But there was no time to apologise for the pemmican. Bill caught the horses and brought them over. Seth handed the girl up on to the pad-saddle of the black horse. She looked down at him. "Aren't you going to ride?"

"After a while," he said, adding nothing more but striking out ahead of the animals, breaking trail through the growing drifts.

Bill Williams was hunched over more than ever. With the buffalo robe up over his head and snugged in so that little showed beyond his hatchet features, he looked more grotesque than ever. His thin lips moved constantly although no sound came out, and his little eyes shone with a ferret-like worry.

By the time they were back down into the little valley their tracks behind them were obliterated. Bill twisted like an injured crane, and looked back. He flicked a glance at the girl. She was covered like he was with the second buffalo robe. Her breath came in short spurts of steam. He swung back forward and called out to Seth.

"You danged idiot. Why'n't you fetch along another horse?"

Seth hesitated. From behind him Karin's clear voice rang out.

"Why not ride up along with me, Seth? Guess there's less weight for the horse if you share with me rather than with old Bill."

Though it was what he had half-hoped for, he didn't know how to say yes. So he just loped back and swung up behind her.

Bill mumbled and cursed under his breath. The horses didn't need guiding and at least he could keep his hands warm within the robe. Bill's disagreeable little beast forged ahead. Karin's black horse followed Bill's animal. Like that they fought their way through interminable dark hours until all of them had lost track of time and weren't sure whether it was late evening or night.

Seth had no buffalo robe. He was conscious of a growing exhaustion. That and the slicing, freezing cold. He blinked at Bill's scrawny features with the hoar-frost rimming them on the buffalo fur, and laughed.

"You're a sight, Bill." Williams mumbled something Seth didn't hear. He ignored the whining sound anyway. "Know where you are now?" Bill nodded bleakly, saying nothing. "Ride on then. We'll follow you for a while."

Bill drummed on the little horse's skinny ribs and for the first few seconds got nothing more than some angry tail-swishing and an ear-back toss of the ugly head. He kicked harder and began to swear at the animal. Then it moved out reluctantly, bucking the shallower drifts of the trail.

Now Karin and Seth on their black horse were bringing up the rear. Strangely, they seemed cut off from the bobbing figure who picked a precarious way through the drifts ahead of them. The girl reached down impulsively and found his icy fist on the reins. He glanced round and smiled at her. The snow was blanket thick around them and swirling faster. It was like a thick curtain ringing them round in a private world.

"Seth? Why did you do it, Seth?"

"I'll show you when we get back," he said. "Jules has my parfleche pouch. There's something in it. I'll show you."

Mystified and showing it clearly, she looked at him with a wide-eyed look. "But why don't you tell me?"

He flashed her a ruddy smile then turned back to the trail. "I'm not very good at tellin' things like this. In fact, I never did it before. Anyway, it'll save."

Her perplexity didn't vanish, but it softened a little before she asked the next question. "Is my father all right?"

"I reckon," he said without looking round. "I didn't see him but he came back with Jules. He'll be drawed out, I expect. They had about as bad a trip of it as we did."

She nodded a little. It was hard to tell whether she did it purposefully or whether her head was just bobbing in time with the black horse's plodding gait. "Was it you killed Plume?"

"Yes. He came with four other Bloods. I killed Plume in a fair fight an' the others are prisoners. They'll be turned loose and sent back as soon as this storm lifts." He turned and looked at her. "Where were you and your paw going when the Injuns hit your party?"

"To California. Daddy heard there was a big demand for doctors out there."

"Uh," Seth said. He travelled along for several miles before he spoke again. "Karin, this is pretty country. Some day there'll be lots of folks in here."

"Yes," she said, wonderingly. "I suppose so. It *is* pretty. Moon Prairie is beautiful. Have you ever seen it when the snow wasn't on it?"

"No, but I'd like to. I'll go back there some day."

Her fingers tightened on his. "Why?"

He didn't look up. "Because that's where I finally saw you. Really saw you, I mean."

She was frowning but he didn't know it. Something up ahead had stopped Bill in his tracks. He let go of the stirrup-leather and was starting forward when he heard the familiar voice of old Jules.

"That you, Bill? You've got Seth and the girl?"

"Yeh," Bill shouted against the milky flakes that swirled over larger between him and the dim shapes he saw ahead. "That you, Jules?"

"Yeh. I got to worryin'. This here's a real blizzard. You kin smell 'em."

"Smell hell," Bill called back disgustedly. "No one but a idiot'd be out in such weather. We close to home, Jules?"

"Nigh on there." He materialised beside them out of the wilderness of falling flakes. " 'Lo, Seth. Looks like you found her." His head bent forward and he peered at Karin. "Well, young lady," he said approvingly, "that's sure a more come-alive face than the last one I saw you a-wearin'."

Then his glance dropped to Seth's hand on the reins. Karin's fingers still covered it. Under old Jules's peering gaze her grasp loosened, and Seth was overwhelmed by a sense of impending loss. But then, next moment, her fingers tightened their hold again and he heard her reply, firmly though laughingly given.

"I guess I've got something to look come-alive about, Jules."

Jules smiled widely, knowingly. He cocked an eye at Seth.

"I reckon," he said.

"Jules, you got my pouch with you?"

"Sure. You want it?"

"Later," Seth said. "When we get home. It'll keep till then."

A thoroughly exasperated and angered old Bill Williams rode up alongside them. "God a'mighty, folks. Hear me now—this here's a blizzard. Come on, won't you, please, afore you're buried for all time in it?"

The other three shared a little laugh of good-humoured tolerance, but old Bill only snorted and led the way on. Nothing was said after that until they were mushing down the little incline towards the Three Forks. By then they were using all their energy and breath to fight the snow, and Karin, only recently—and partially—recovered from a gruelling ordeal, needed Seth's help to dismount at the tipi. His arms went about her naturally, as if she belonged there. He kept one arm round her waist as they stooped and entered the warm, food-fragrant shelter.

And there sat Dr. Baird, leaner by some pounds than

153

when Seth had last seen him. He leapt to his feet at Karin's entrance. She left the protective circle of Seth's arm and ran to her father. The older man's glance went directly to Seth's face over her shoulder.

"Thank you," he said. In its grand simplicity it had a dignity that a spate of words would have lacked. There was after all more to the man than a medical degree and a concern for his own skin. He had breeding and endurance. Seth found himself respecting him.

He nodded acceptance of the proffered thanks and turned to the soup pot steaming on the fire. He found suddenly that the warmth and the smell of food made him weak—deathly tired and weak. He'd been employed at full stretch for some little time now, he told himself. Better sit down before he fell down.

He barely made it to the stool by the fire. As he slumped down on it Karin's hand was on his shoulder.

"Let me," she said. "I'll fix you something to eat."

He nodded dumbly. She made no move to pick up the bouillon ladle. Instead she dropped to her knees beside him.

"Oh, Seth," she said.

It was all there, in her voice.

Old Jules, who had come in and silently witnessed the whole scene, emitted a dry chuckle.

"Have to get old Bill's squaw fix us up some new clothes for the wedding, I reckon," he said.

"Wedding?" It was Dr. Baird, puzzled, confused, staring at his daughter as she knelt by Seth's side.

"Looks like a wedding to me," Jules observed. "Can't think of any other reason he'd go to so much trouble to hook her out of a Blackfoot wickiup. What d'you say, Baird?"

The man didn't know what to say. Gratitude he could offer to this strange young man from the wildest frontier, but kinship—?

154

"Karin?" he said, uncertainly. "You hear this?"

She half-turned her head. "I heard him, father." She turned back to Seth. "You haven't said anything, Seth."

She was gazing up into his face, earnest, imploring. He found the haze of fatigue slowly clearing before the fire of those violet-blue eyes.

"Why, Karin—you know I don't have much truck with words. But I think I can show you." He held out his hand to Jules without taking his eyes off Karin's face. "The pouch, Jules."

It was put into his hands. Without taking a glance at anyone else's expression he felt in the beaded bag and brought out the miniature. He held it out to Karin.

Like one in a trance she accepted it, gazed down at it where it lay cradled in her two palms. "Where did you get this?" she whispered.

"Found it where you were ambushed by the Blackfeet, Karin. That's why I had to find you. That's why I had to get you away from the Bloods. That's why I had to kill Plume. And that's—that's the whole story."

"Not quite," was her soft answer. "Which will you have, Seth? The picture or the reality?"

He blinked away the last remains of weariness. With one broad hand, suddenly grown mighty gentle, he pushed the miniature that she was holding out to him until it tilted and fell off her palm. Then he curled his fingers about hers.

Jules cleared his throat. "Now, Medicine Man," he demanded, "what d'you say to that?"

Baird fetched out a quaint rag of a handkerchief and blew his nose roughly.

"There doesn't seem much I can say," he observed, though in a rather husky voice. "This young fellow seems to get everything he goes after. And if Karin's sure it isn't just gratitude. . . .?"

"Gratitude?" Karin echoed. "Why, that's silly. I agreed to his wild scheme of escape because I thought if I had to

155

die, I'd rather die with him than with anyone else in the world. I thought he was leading me straight to my death! And even then, I loved him."

Jules picked up the miniature and took Baird by the arm. "Let's you and me go," he said slyly, "and show this here work of art to old Bill, in his lodge. I'm certain he'd appreciate it. And at the same time we can ask his squaw about a new suit of buckskins for the wedding."

They went out quietly, drawing the flap close behind them.

But the two left within the tipi never even heard them go.

Lauran Paine who, under his own name and various pseudonyms has written over 900 books, was born in Duluth, Minnesota, a descendant of the Revolutionary War patriot and author, Thomas Paine. His family moved to California when he was at an early age and his apprenticeship as a Western writer came about through the years he spent in the livestock trade, rodeos, and even motion pictures where he served as an extra because of his expert horsemanship in several films starring movie cowboy Johnny Mack Brown. In the late 1930s, Paine trapped wild horses in Northern Arizona and even, for a time, worked as a professional farrier. Paine came to know the Old West through the eyes of many who had been born in the previous century and he learned that Western life had been very different from the way it was portrayed on the screen. "I knew men who had killed other men," he later recalled. "But they were the exceptions. Prior to and during the Depression, people were just too busy eking out an existence to indulge in Saturday-night brawls." He served in the U.S. Navy in the Second World War and began writing for Western pulp magazines following his discharge. It is interesting to note that all of his earliest novels (written under his own name and the pseudonym Mark Carrel) were published in the British market and he soon had as strong a following in that country as in the United States. Paine's Western fiction is characterized by strong plots, authenticity, an apparently effortless ability to construct situation and character, and a preference for building his stories upon a solid foundation of historical fact. *Adobe Empire* (1956), one of his best novels, is a fictionalized account of the last twenty years in the life of trader William Bent and, in an off-trail way, has a melancholy, bittersweet texture that is not easily forgotten. *Moon Prairie* (1950), first published in the United States in 1994, is a memorable story set during the mountain man period of the frontier. In later novels such as *The Homesteaders* (1986) or *The Open Range Men* (1990), he showed that the special magic and power of his stories and characters had only matured along with his basic themes of changing times, changing attitudes, learning from experience, respecting nature, and the yearning for a simpler, more moderate way of life. His most recent Western novels include *Tears of the Heart*, *Lockwood* and *The White Bird*.